BOOKS BY
BARBARA HAWORTH-ATTARD

Dark of the Moon
The Three Wishbells
TruthSinger
Home Child
Buried Treasure
WyndMagic
Love-Lies-Bleeding

FLYING GEESE

Barbara Haworth-Attard

Flying Geese

Best wishes!

Barbara Haworth-Attard

HarperCollins*Publishers*Ltd

Flying Geese
Copyright © 2001 by Barbara Haworth-Attard.
All rights reserved. No part of this book may be used or reproduced in any manner whatsoever without prior written permission except in the case of brief quotations embodied in reviews.
For information address
HarperCollins Publishers Ltd,
55 Avenue Road, Suite 2900,
Toronto, Ontario, Canada M5R 3L2

www.harpercanada.com

HarperCollins books may be purchased for educational, business, or sales promotional use. For information please write: Special Markets Department, HarperCollins Canada, 55 Avenue Road, Suite 2900, Toronto, Ontario, Canada M5R 3L2

First HarperCollins trade paper ed.
ISBN 0-00-648573-1

Thank you to Judy Ann Sadler for her sharing of her craft expertise, and to the staff of the London Room and the London Public Library for always finding an answer to my questions.

Thank you to the Ontario Arts Council for a grant provided to the author.

Canadian Cataloguing in Publication Data

Haworth-Attard, Barbara, 1953–
Flying geese

ISBN 0-00-648573-1

I. Title

PS8565.A865F59 2001   jC813'.54
C00-932365-1
PZ7.H38Fl 2001

01 02 03 04 HC 4 3 2 1

Printed and bound in the United States
Set in Monotype Plantin

For the London Friendship Quilters' Guild
for their caring and laughter

Contents

Author's Note

A main thread in this book is the Flying Geese quilt Margaret is working on. Textile history is an important aspect of history that is often overlooked. Quilts were important, non-written historical records of women's particular and personal insights. At the end of a long day, a pioneer woman, living in harsh isolation, would arrange patches in eye-pleasing designs. This work offered a break from endless chores, colour in a drab world, and an opportunity to socialize. For many it also offered the only outlet they had for creative expression. Today, the quilting tradition remains strong as patterns are handed down from generation to generation and women, and also many men, continue to stitch their hopes and sorrows and joys into these material labours of love.

While I have made every effort to present a historically accurate picture of London, Ontario, in 1915, I would ask the reader to remember that this is a work of fiction and the characters are wholly a product of my imagination.

For more information on quilting and the First World War era, visit my website at:

www.barbarahaworthattard.com

FLYING GEESE

Chapter 1

Margaret heard their cry first: a single, flat *honk*, then others joining, filling the air with sound. She squinted into the late afternoon sun to see geese fly low over the Saskatchewan prairie in an orderly V-formation. Wings beat strong and heads strained southward. Summer was over.

Every year she and her father would watch the geese arrive in the soft, spring nights and leave in the crisp air of fall. Margaret was comfortable with the geese going, sure in the knowledge they would return. Except this year—this year she was sure of nothing.

"Margaret Brown! Stop your dreaming and bring in the wash from the line," her mother ordered through the kitchen window.

Worry gnawing at her insides, Margaret pulled pegs from the sheets, momentarily wrestling the wind for the billowing cotton. She folded haphazardly before stuffing them into a woven basket. She continued along the clothesline until she came to the quilt airing at the end. Her own Flower Basket quilt. She stopped and stood back to admire its soft yellow, blue, and green hues. Grandma Brown had made it special for her a year ago, finishing it six months before a stroke had carried her away to her final resting place, as Mama called heaven.

Margaret closed her eyes and buried her head in its colourful folds, hearing her grandmother's voice. *I'm quilting spring for you, Grandgirl.* She missed Grandma Brown dreadfully, especially now when everything was so upset. Seeing the elderly woman's back bent over her wooden quilting frame in the parlour had a way of steadying them all. Was she enjoying her final resting place? Margaret wondered. She'd never actually seen her grandmother rest. She kept busy from dawn to long past dark, working in the garden, canning and preserving, cooking and washing. In her spare moments, out would come scraps of material from her apron pocket and she'd sew. Maybe heaven was doing what you liked best and for Grandma Brown, that was piecing and quilting. She certainly was not resting.

And what was heaven for herself? Margaret wondered. Perhaps yellow sun on her skin, blue sky above, wind on her cheeks, and her feet carrying her so swiftly the brown prairie grass blurred beneath them. Certainly not hanging the wash.

With a sigh, Margaret straightened and ran her fingers over the swirling feather stitching on the quilt, feeling the love embedded with the thread—and also a moment's pride. Some of the stitches in the quilt were her own—Grandma Brown had finally declared Margaret skilled enough to take a place with the women seated around the frame during what was to be her grandmother's last quilting bee. *You come quilt now, Grandgirl. Even stitches, child. Don't dig in the needle; ply it gently.*

She'd accompanied Grandma Brown to quilting bees since she was very young, sitting many an afternoon within a small house, the roof above her the quilt top stretched taut on its frame; the walls, women's skirt-clad legs and booted feet. Reluctantly she now pulled the quilt from the line, smelling the freshness of an afternoon outside, and wished once more to be within that safe, small haven.

Settling the basket on one hip, Margaret moved towards the house. She shivered as the sun hid behind grey clouds gathering on the horizon and the growing darkness stole warmth and light. She recalled another afternoon three weeks ago, the sky clear except for one boiling black thunderhead herded by an unusually warm wind directly to their fields. Watching the cloud from the kitchen, Dad had said a spot of rain would be good for the crop, but suddenly the sky yellowed and wind roared. The drumming on the roof deafened them as hailstones the size of eggs fell on the house and fields. She'd watched her father's expression become grimmer with each passing minute, and though the storm rapidly took its leave, the bleakness on his face had not.

Margaret kept her eyes on the dirt path to the porch steps, unable to look upon the battered ruins of their grain. The neighbours had come shortly after, shaking their heads over the whims of nature and God that left only the Brown farm damaged. Everyone else had a bumper crop this harvest and, due to the war which had caused a shortage of wheat in Europe, prices were at an all time high. All the families around them had more money than they knew what to do with—all except the Browns. Margaret passed through the porch and into the kitchen.

"Did you shake those sheets well and smooth the wrinkles out?" Mrs. Brown asked.

"Yes, Mama," Margaret replied, hoping she had. She couldn't remember, she'd been so caught up in her own misery.

"You can help Evie with the vegetables then." Her mother settled down in a chair and picked up a pair of overalls and a needle and thread.

Margaret crossed to the work table where her older sister stood peeling potatoes. Potatoes for breakfast, lunch, and supper. That and carrots and squash, the only vegetables left in Mama's garden. She looked at them with distaste, but said nothing. Mama's hand was quick to reach out and strike these days, and they were all learning fast to hold their tongues.

Evie smiled at her, well aware of her thoughts. Margaret picked up a knife, then stole a look at her mother. Head bent, her needle winked silver in and out of George's overalls. More patches than pants, Margaret thought, but there was no money for clothes. Hadn't been any since the last decent harvest three years ago.

"You're taking half the potato with the peel," Evie scolded. "Be careful."

"I was just taking out an eye," Margaret protested.

Her mother folded the mended pants, stood, and groaned, arching her back until Margaret could see the small bulge of the new baby under her dress. That would make seven children altogether: her brothers, Edward, seventeen, and George, nearly eleven, in the fields with Dad, and the three-year-old twins, Timothy and Taylor, blessedly asleep for once; her sister Evie, fourteen; and Margaret, turned twelve last week.

She watched apprehensively as her mother pulled a sheet from the basket and shook it out, clicking her tongue in annoyance at the deep creases. Mrs. Brown glanced sharply at Margaret, eyes blazing a moment, then quickly dulling. "The hem's come down on this one," she said wearily. "You could mend it before supper."

Margaret nodded and wiped her hands on a towel. She rummaged through the sewing basket for needle and thread, seated herself, and began to hem neatly.

"I will say," her mother remarked, peering over Margaret's shoulder, "your stitches are tidy."

Margaret felt pride at her mother's words, which immediately faded as Mama continued. "They're the only thing tidy about you. How you get in such a state between breakfast and supper is beyond me."

Conscious of the unruly strands of yellow hair escaping

from her braid, Margaret quickly shifted the sheet on her lap to hide the long streak of black grease left on her skirt from helping Edward oil the wagon wheels before he'd gone to town. He was patient like that, Edward was. Showing her how things went together and worked. Maybe that was why she liked piecing, too. Liked the way the patches went together so well. She glanced up to see Mama's blue eyes on her, prairie sky eyes her dad called them, reborn in Margaret's face. Her mother raised her eyebrows and Margaret knew she'd seen the stain, but was letting it go this time. That worried her more than if Mama had slapped her for her carelessness.

All of a sudden, Mrs. Brown reached out and gently tucked a curl behind Margaret's ear. "You'll lose your sight sewing with that hair in your eyes," she said.

Margaret studied her mother's face, anxiously noting the thin cheeks and purple smudges under her eyes. She'd heard her parents talking late the night before as they often did now and had crept from her bed to sit at the top of the stairs to listen.

It was a well-worn discussion, turned over and inside out: the hail storm, Dad's accident, the lack of harvest, the lack of money, the lack of food. Except, a month ago, new words had been added. Words that scared Margaret.

"Harold says we should come to Ontario," Mama said. Mother's brother, Uncle Harold, she meant. "You can't work the farm with your back the way it is. He says we could stay with him and Dot until we get settled."

"I don't take charity from another man," her father replied.

"Just like you won't take the help offered by the other farmers. You can't leave all the work to Edward and George. They can't do it. You should look to your pride," Mama snapped angrily. Then, after a moment, "Harold says you could get a job."

"What kind of job?" Dad asked. "I don't know anything but farming."

"He said you could get a job in a store or an office. Something where your bad back won't matter."

Dad *hhmmphed* at that. "There's nothing wrong with the farm. We'll make a living from it."

"How?" Mama said flatly. "The doctor says you'll never be able to lift again. The boys can't do it by themselves, and we can't afford to hire a man."

They were silent so long Margaret had crawled back into bed and curled up under her quilt next to Evie.

She sat now, needle unmoving between thumb and forefinger as she remembered Dad's accident. A year September it had been, while bringing in the last of the harvest. It had been a poor one, as had been the year's before, with prices so low Dad had grumbled it wasn't even worth hauling to the grain elevators. She'd been watching as Edward backed up the wagon piled high with hay, the bale rising to the hay mow and a gust of wind coming from nowhere, swinging it wide. Dad, standing in the hay-mow window, leaned forward to grab it and suddenly toppled over, falling heavily on his back in the dirt. Two weeks in hospital, six months bedridden, five months hobbling about, and a final doctor's pronouncement that the back was as good as it would ever be. Not good enough to farm.

"Some geese flew over," she said suddenly, more to keep her thoughts at bay than to tell Evie and her mother. "Leaving for the winter, but I guess they'll be back come spring." *But will I be here to see them?* She wanted to ask that question so badly it hurt, but was just as badly scared to hear the answer, so she said nothing. Perhaps silence would make them forget Ontario.

Margaret held the sheet to the window to catch the fast-fading light and studied the hem. A satisfied smile played about her lips. She had done a nice mending job. She liked sewing: enjoyed the feel of material beneath her fingers, rough or smooth, enjoyed the rhythm of the needle going in and out. It settled her mind somehow. She and her best friend, Catherine, had made patchwork quilts for their dolls this past summer from scraps Catherine's mother gave them. As always, she had been fascinated with the way the small pieces were cleverly sewn together in a larger pattern. She took after her Grandma Brown that way, Mama said, always playing with bits of material.

Voices in the yard warned of the arrival of her father and George for supper.

"They're in early. Set the table," Mama called from the bedroom where she was coaxing Timothy and Taylor to use the chamber pot. "And. . ." She paused, considering. "It's getting dull. Light a lamp. Just one, mind."

Margaret hurried to set dishes on the table. Lifting a round lid off the stove, she put in a piece of straw, waited until it flamed, then carried it to the lamp's wick. Just one. Mama was being careful with most things these days. Waste not, want not. The door to the kitchen opened and her father walked in with his stiff gait, legacy of the fall. George followed, carrying a pail of milk that he set carefully down by the indoor pump.

Margaret put a plate of pork on the table, noticing how her sister had sliced it thinly and spread it out to look like more. She placed a loaf of brown bread and a knife by her father's plate and butter, a luxury they enjoyed as her mother insisted they keep a cow for milk for the twins. A steaming bowl of the ever-present potatoes was set at the opposite end. Shooing Timothy and Taylor from the bedroom, Mrs. Brown rushed to and from the stove. Margaret plopped Timothy on his chair at the table, knowing his twin, Taylor, would follow. That was the way with twins, Margaret had long ago decided; one led, the other followed. Who did what they somehow sorted out between themselves.

From outside she heard the rattle of wagon wheels over the rutted lane and Edward's voice halting the horses. A few minutes later the porch door slammed as he came in. Margaret slid into her chair, her eyes on the red flush staining her older brother's cheeks. Just the wind giving him high colour, she assured herself, but her stomach twisted suddenly, like it did when a storm was brewing. If you want to know the weather, Dad often joked, ask after Margaret's stomach.

"I got the mail in town." Edward dropped a handful of letters by his father's plate before dragging out a chair and flopping into it. He shot a quick glance at the table, then uttered a dismayed, "Potatoes."

Margaret bent her head and covered a small smile.

"It's good, filling food," Mrs. Brown scolded. "You should be happy to be eating at all. You didn't wash," she reminded him.

Edward pumped water into a basin and splashed it over his face, neck, and hands. He grabbed a towel, mopped up the drops, and threw it carelessly on a chair. Like she would do, Margaret thought. Evie would have folded it neatly. In fact, everything about Evie was neat, from her small feet, tidy brown hair, and spotless apron to the way she peeled potatoes.

Crossing back to his chair, he grabbed one of Margaret's braids and gave it a sharp tug, grinning when he caught her eye. He was surely excited about something.

Mr. Brown tore open an envelope and pulled out a letter, face clouding over as he read the contents. "Thieves! The lot of them. Out to get a man's last penny!" he exploded.

"Martin," Mrs. Brown chided gently. "We're having supper. Can't that wait?"

Absently, Margaret's father nodded, threw down the letter, scooped potatoes from a bowl, and speared a piece of meat.

"There was a rally at the Agriculture offices today," Edward began. "For the war effort."

Timothy began to wail, tossing his carrots to the floor. Margaret impatiently shushed him and scrambled on the kitchen floor to pick up the vegetables, alert to the careful note in Edward's voice. Something important coming, she knew.

"A man all the way from Ottawa was talking. A doctor and a reverend both," Edward marvelled. "I didn't catch his name. He said every Canadian, every man, woman, and child, must have a part in the struggle for freedom from oppression." Edward's voice took on the man's sombre tones.

George watched him avidly, though Margaret noticed it didn't interrupt his fork going up and down from plate to mouth.

"More war talk," Mrs. Brown said, voice taut. "It's over there, in Europe, it doesn't affect us."

"But it does, Mama," Edward protested. "We're part of the British Empire and all Canada's young manhood must answer the call to fight."

Repeating the man again, Margaret guessed. Edward didn't know words like that. Like herself, he hadn't been the best student at their tiny school. Evie was the scholar in the family.

"Martin, the blessing." Mrs. Brown bowed her head but not before Margaret saw the worry in her eyes. Mama felt something bad coming, too.

Edward continued. "He said we must struggle for liberty and righteousness to prevail so Germany does not triumph." Silence. Then, "I joined up, Mama. I signed my attestation papers this afternoon. I'm part of the 46th Infantry Battalion. I have to report to Moose Jaw in three days for my training. Christian Ashford joined, too."

"Martin! The blessing!" Mrs. Brown repeated, voice higher and tinged with fear.

Margaret closed her eyes, waited until her father cleared his throat, then opened them to find Edward staring back at her. Excitement struggled with fear in his eyes, but his mouth was set stubborn. No matter what Mama said, he'd be going away to war.

"Lord," Mr. Brown began. "Thank you for the abundance . . ." he paused a moment, ". . . of trouble . . ."

"Martin!" Mrs. Brown admonished.

Margaret's eyes flew to her father's bowed head.

". . . that's all we've had lately, Lord. Trouble, and we need a miracle to survive," he continued. "Though there has been a shortage of miracles around here lately."

"Martin," Margaret's mother exclaimed again. "What kind of a blessing is that!"

Mr. Brown thumped his fist on the table. "There's been no harvest for two years, Olivia, then finally I get a bumper crop and hail wipes it out. And this . . ." He grabbed the letter sitting beside his plate and waved it in the air. "It's the bank telling me they are foreclosing on the farm as we owe money for seed and equipment and I can't pay it back. And there's other bills. We still have to pay the doctor and the hospital . . ." He stood abruptly and his chair crashed to the floor. Timothy began to wail. Taylor immediately joined him. "And now Edward's going off who knows where to fight in a war," he shouted over the crying. "I can't run the farm alone."

"Dad. I'm sorry." Edward's face was stricken. "I guess I wasn't really thinking . . ."

"No," his father interrupted. "You're a man now. You do what you have to do."

Margaret pulled Timothy from his chair and joggled him up and down on her knee. "Dad, I can help farm. I'm getting bigger now. I'm even stronger than George."

George looked at her in disgust. "You aren't stronger than me and girls don't farm," he told her.

"Sure they do," Margaret argued. Timothy grabbed a stray piece of hair and pulled hard, bringing tears to her eyes. She quickly dumped him on Evie.

Evie yelped. "Don't put him on me. He's all wet!"

"I've helped in the fields before," Margaret protested, ignoring Evie.

"Helping is not the same as real farming," George told her.

"Margaret, take him back! He's soaking. He's ruining my dress." Evie held Timothy away from her skirt.

"Enough!" Mr. Brown roared. He limped to the porch door. Yanking it open, he stopped and spoke into the sudden silence. "Olivia, start packing. We're going to Ontario."

Chapter 2

Margaret sat, her back against the kitchen wall and knees drawn to her chest, trying to shut out the voices from the yard. It was disturbing having people going over her family's belongings, knowing in a few hours Evie's and her bed would be in someone else's house, other people sleeping on it. Just as disturbing was the bare kitchen, stripped of table and chairs, even Mama's corner cabinet Dad had built special to hold her few precious pieces of china. Except for some pots and pans and plates that could fit into suitcases or be easily carried, everything was up for auction, the money needed for train tickets to Ontario.

She held tight to her quilt and a large bag of Grandma Brown's remnants of material, fearful even they might be torn from her arms and sold. Occasionally, she would finger a triangle or square in the quilt, taking comfort in the memory of her grandmother's voice. *That light blue is from a dress I had as a young girl. Your grandpa said it was that dress matching my eyes that made him decide to marry me. You put it in a quilt someday, Grandgirl. Maybe it will bring you good luck and a handsome man, too.* Margaret remembered blushing at that.

The past two weeks had been a rush of packing, arranging the auction, and Edward leaving for the army. He was out there now in the yard in his brown uniform, given leave from the camp to return home to say goodbye to them before they left for Ontario the following morning.

"Margaret? Where are you?" Her friend, Catherine, banged into the kitchen, peered around its dim interior until she spotted Margaret, then flopped down beside her.

"You're really going then?" she cried.

Margaret nodded.

"I didn't think it true until I got here and saw all the people at the auction. Dad's here for the corner cabinet for Mother. He says your father's carpentry is second to none." She paused, taking in Margaret's sad face. "Oh, sorry," she apologized. "I wasn't thinking."

Most of the people out there weren't thinking, Margaret thought angrily. Friends, neighbours, church folk—all rudely pawing through their possessions and discussing the value like her family had gone already and been forgotten.

"Grandmother has sent me some new dress patterns," Catherine chattered. She spread them over the kitchen floor. "I brought them to show you. Mother and I are making this one first."

Margaret glanced down at the pattern her friend thrust into her hands. It was a lovely dress made up in green wool with a lace collar to finish it.

"It's beautiful," she said. Her hand shook as she handed it back, suddenly aware of the worn material in her skirt, the white lines where the hem had been turned down as far as it could go. She was shooting up like a weed, Mama said, sighing, making Margaret feel like she'd done something bad by growing. She was already Evie's height, so there were no more hand-me-downs left for her. Her sturdiness was the Wallace side of the family, Grandma Brown had often told her. Margaret took after her grandmother's mother's people: solidly built to work well in the fields. And those same people had passed on skilled hands that made tidy stitches, Grandma Brown had added. A stab of envy went through Margaret as she fingered Catherine's patterns. She'd never had a new dress that was just her own.

She leaned her head back against the wall, suddenly exhausted. She loved her friend dearly, but today Catherine's chatter grated on her ears. Fighting back tears, she pretended to study the patterns, when suddenly the edge of one caught her eye. She burrowed a hand beneath the pile and pulled it out.

"*Flying Geese Quilt*," she read. "Did your grandmother send you this too?"

Catherine glanced over, then quickly away, uninterested. "Yes, but I'm looking for . . ." She rifled through the patterns. "Where is that adorable blouse?"

Margaret studied the orderly rows of V-shaped patchwork. They looked exactly like the geese flying over her house, but with material rather than feathers.

"Here it is," Catherine crowed. With a last, longing look, Margaret put the Flying Geese pattern down.

"Margaret." Evie poked her head in the door. "Mama wants you to watch Taylor and Timothy. The auction is about to start, and she doesn't want them bothering people. I have to help bundle up the linen."

Margaret climbed to her feet.

"And straighten your hair. You look like you just got out of bed," Evie added.

Margaret stuck her tongue out at her sister, then ran quickly upstairs and pushed her quilt and Grandma's remnant bag into a corner behind her satchel, packed and waiting to go. Hopefully, the bag would be safe from the auction there.

Back in the yard, she rounded up the twins. "Play, Margaret," Taylor shouted. She tossed him a rag ball.

"Edward looks quite handsome," Catherine whispered into her ear.

Margaret looked around the yard until she saw her brother leaning casually against the fence, crisp uniform shouting new. Handsome, yes, but with his thin build—small bones from the Brown side of the family—he looked like a little boy dressed in his father's clothes. She didn't recognize him anymore in that uniform. Her Edward wore overalls and pulled her braids and teased her. Not unkindly like her classmates did last year when she shot up over even the tallest boys in her school, but in a gentle, laughing way. This new Edward in uniform was a stranger. Men slapped him on the back and shook his hand. Moving closer, Margaret heard one say, "Congratulations, young fellow. Wish I was younger so I could go myself. Hate missing all the excitement."

George swaggered after his older brother, imitating his casual pose, hands in pockets and beaming as if he were the new soldier going off to war. Mama, too, was watching Edward, Margaret saw, eyes sadly following him around the yard. Why were the men so pleased to see him leave, she wondered, and the women sympathetically patting Mama on the shoulder and her looking ready to burst into tears?

Why did he have to go to a war so far away? Just because they were part of the British Empire didn't seem reason enough to go over the ocean to Europe. She wished now she'd listened more closely to their teacher, Mr. Johnson, reading from the newspaper when the war started last year. August of 1914 that had been. She remembered it had to do with some countries called the Balkans, and the Germans, and a duke who had been assassinated, but she'd found it all so confusing she'd paid scant attention.

Mr. Murphy, Catherine's father, came up and reached behind Margaret's ear. "Look what I found here!" he exclaimed. With a huge grin he handed her a copper penny. "I guess it's yours, young lady."

With a weak smile Margaret took the coin. Cheeks perpetually red, lips always smiling, Mr. Murphy's bulk strained the buttons of his railroad guard's uniform. Margaret didn't think she'd ever seen Catherine's father without a smile. She watched her own father make his way through the crowd with his awkward limp. When was the last time a smile had lit his gaunt face and erased lines etched deep from sun, work, and worry? Perhaps the difference was Mr. Murphy had a steady paying job on the railroad and only Catherine to worry about, while her dad had a whole farm, six-nearly-seven children, and a bad back.

The auction began in earnest and Margaret watched the kitchen table go, followed by Mama's rocking chair. The chickens and cranky rooster, the cow bawling its protest, and the horse, skittish from the noise, went quickly. As the afternoon wore on wagons pulled away from the house to the main road, new purchases tied securely in back, until there was only Mama's cupboard left.

"We will begin the bidding at ten dollars for this fine piece of craftsmanship," the auctioneer announced.

Mr. Murphy immediately put up his hand.

"Wait! Wait!" Margaret's father made his way to the front of the small crowd. "I'm sorry, folks. That piece is not for sale. It's going with us."

Margaret saw her mother put her hand to her mouth, surprise widening her eyes. With murmurs of disappointment, the crowd thinned. Margaret's father came up to Mr. Murphy. "Sorry about the confusion. I know you came for that piece in particular, but Olivia has her heart set on keeping it."

Mr. Murphy smiled and waved a hand in the air. "Not to worry."

Margaret's mother came up. "We could have got good money for the cupboard," she said in a low, anxious voice. "Heaven knows we could use it."

"We don't have to sell the very life in us," Margaret's father said abruptly, then turned back to Mr. Murphy. "I wonder if I might ask a favour of you. I'd like to take the cupboard down to the train station right away and see about having it shipped to Ontario and . . ." He looked around the yard as if surprised to see it empty. ". . . I don't have a wagon anymore."

"We'll drop Catherine at home first, then head to town," Mr. Murphy assured him. He closed one eye in an exaggerated wink. "I might be able to get you a good rate, being a railroad man and all."

"I'm obliged. I'll have Edward and George put it in the wagon then, while I speak to the auctioneer and get settled up with him."

Margaret held out a small piece of paper to Catherine. "This is my Uncle Harold's address. Will you write to me?"

"Of course I'll write." Catherine's voice wobbled.

"It'll only be for a short while," Margaret went on. "Another year George and I will be grown enough to help with the farm and then we'll be back." After all, she had a solid Wallace build that could work well. Grandma Brown had said so.

She caught Mr. Murphy's puzzled eyes on her, but stubbornly ignored him. They would be back. Like the geese.

Catherine suddenly leafed through the sewing patterns and shoved one into Margaret's hands. "I want you to have this as a goodbye gift."

The Flying Geese quilt! Margaret squeezed Catherine's hand, unable to speak.

They stood side by side watching Edward and George wrestle the cupboard over the wagon tail. Mrs. Brown handed them blankets to wrap it in, with instructions to make sure it was secure. Finally, it was done to her satisfaction and they jumped down from the wagon.

"I'll be going into town with Dad and Mr. Murphy," Edward announced. "I have to catch the train back to camp."

Margaret felt her heart sink. First Edward, then them leaving. She stared down at her feet, feeling as if the very earth beneath her was eroding away. Where would she stand then? She headed quickly for the house and upstairs to

Evie's and her bedroom, lowered herself to the floor, and hugged Grandma's ragbag to her chest.

"Margaret!" Edward called but she didn't answer. A moment later he appeared in the doorway.

"Weren't you going to say goodbye to me?"

She shrugged.

Edward squatted down beside her. "Just imagine. I've never seen anything but prairie all my life and soon I'll be going straight across Canada, then over the ocean! What an adventure."

Margaret tried but could not imagine an endless stretch of water, an ocean. She'd only known land, the prairie. She gripped his arm until her knuckles showed white. "Mama says you're too young to be a soldier. You're only seventeen."

"I'll be eighteen in two months. Dad says I'm a man. Besides, it's my duty to go. You wouldn't want me called a coward." She wasn't sure if he was trying to convince her or himself.

"There's men fighting over there on the Western Front," he added. "Fighting for us so we don't become a German colony. I have to go help."

Put that way, Margaret almost wished she was a boy so she could go, too. Almost. She scrambled to her feet. "Dad says it'll be over soon. Maybe even before you finish your training and you won't go over the ocean at all."

Edward swung her off her feet. "I hope not. I don't want to miss all the fun. Don't get too caught up in those flashy city ways," he teased her.

Margaret squeezed him back fiercely, then stared at him hard.

"Why are you looking cross-eyed?" he demanded.

"I'm remembering what you look like right into my mind, so I don't forget," Margaret told him.

Edward fished in his pocket a moment before holding out

a photograph. "It's me and Christian standing in front of our barracks. Now you don't have to rack your brain with remembering."

"Thanks," Margaret croaked as she took the picture, unable to force words past a huge lump in her throat.

"Now come and give me a proper send-off," Edward told her.

He pulled her down the stairs and into the yard, then climbed into the back of the wagon. Her father heaved himself up beside Mr. Murphy, who clicked to the horses and the wagon swayed to the end of the lane. She watched as it turned down the road, became a tiny black dot against pink-tinged evening clouds, then vanished.

Her mother sighed, wiped her eyes on her apron, then slapped her hands together briskly. "Evie, help me finish the lunches for tomorrow. We'll be making an early start. George, clean up out here and make sure the barn is tidy. I want to go away with a sure mind that the place is neat. I won't have anyone say the Browns left things in a mess. Margaret, keep the twins out from under my feet."

Margaret looked at the picture of Edward and Christian standing in front of a large tent, grinning sheepishly as they squinted into the sun. She placed it carefully in her pocket. It was all she had left of him now.

After a cold supper of bread and pork eaten while sitting on the kitchen floor, Margaret joined her father outside. He stood, one foot on the fence rail, looking over night-blackened fields. The wind bit harsh with a hint of coming frost. She'd be grateful for Grandma's quilt tonight, especially as they were sleeping on the floor. She looked at the white stars littering the sky. Would they hang this low and shine this brightly in Ontario? she wondered.

"How long are we going to stay at Uncle Harold's?" she asked.

"Don't know," Mr. Brown replied shortly. "I got enough

money from the auction to get there and let us live a couple months until I find work. Not enough to get back. Besides . . ." He gestured over the fields. "There's nothing to come back to. The equipment's all gone. I'm leaving debts behind. I'd have to start over again and I'm too old for that."

A tumbleweed rolled across the field, coming to a stop at Margaret's feet. She stepped to one side and let it go on its way. She opened her mouth to tell him her plan to come back when she and George were grown, but a sharp *honk* and the dark shadow of five geese against the night sky made her forget.

"Dad! Look!" She pointed up, but he stared straight ahead, mouth set.

"Does something to you inside, having your whole life spread out for the world to see and realizing there is so little of it," her father said softly and Margaret knew he was speaking to himself. "And now it's gone. It's all gone."

He turned and headed for the house. "Let's hope things are better in Ontario like your Uncle Harold says."

Margaret stood a moment longer, knees trembling. What her grandmother would think of the auction and them leaving, she didn't know. Then she did. Grandma Brown would say, *What has to be has to be; no sense fretting about it,* and she'd pull out her ragbag and begin another quilt. Margaret thought about the Flying Geese pattern tucked safely inside her satchel.

Chapter 3

So this was Ontario, Margaret thought. London, specifically, and even more specifically, Uncle Harold's house. She
trailed behind her two cousins, Pauline and Mary, who were
"acquainting them with the house," as Aunt Dorothy put it.
Pauline was twelve, two years older than Mary, but despite
the age difference they looked like twins in identical navy
serge dresses, white stockings, shiny black shoes, and brown
bobbed hair. They were showing the piano to Evie, who was
making appropriate noises of admiration.

"We also have a Victrola and some music recordings to play
on it . . ." Pauline crossed to the far side of the room and
pointed to a large wooden cabinet next to a couch. ". . . but
you better not wind it because you won't know how it works."

"And this is our telephone," she continued importantly,
moving to the hall. "You speak into this end . . ."

"We do know how to use a telephone," Margaret interrupted.

Evie quickly grabbed her sister's arm and squeezed it
hard. "We had telephones back in Saskatchewan," she told
her cousins. Margaret noticed she didn't elaborate on the
fact that the Brown family did not have their own telephone
but used the general store's.

"I guess we'll show you the bedroom then," Pauline said
with a glare at Margaret.

They filed down the hall towards the kitchen, stepping

over Timothy, who was mashing a half-eaten bread crust into the floor. From upstairs they could hear Taylor whining, fussy from a cold he picked up on the train.

"Your brother is making a mess on our floor," Pauline said.

Evie quickly bent down and picked up the crust. Timothy threw himself full length and banged his heels against the floor. "Mine!" he screamed. Margaret grabbed the bread from Evie and gave it back to him and he quieted immediately, grinding it into the hardwood again.

Pauline sighed exaggeratedly, but continued down the hall.

"Mother likes us to use the back stairs," Mary told them shyly. "The front stairs are only for good company."

Voices filtered into the hall from the kitchen, stopping the girls.

". . . seeing it written in a letter is one thing. Seeing all those children in front of me is something else altogether." Aunt Dorothy's voice came shrill through the closed door.

Uncle Harold's low rumble followed, but Margaret could not make out what he said.

"Well, we can't keep them indefinitely," Aunt Dorothy went on. "We just haven't the room. I had no idea there were so many of them and poor as paupers. That one girl has no shoes! You'd think at the least Olivia could have cleaned them up a bit."

The door swung open and Uncle Harold came out. Margaret felt her face flame as she met his eyes. They'd been on the train for four days and nights, a strange, dreamlike time of hard seats, black soot, and khaki-clad soldiers sitting and lying on the floor or playing cards, all heading to Quebec for training, then catching ships for England.

She'd smoothed her quilt over the wooden train seat so Mama and Dad would be more comfortable, but they all soon tired of sitting upright day and night. Dad let George and her wander the train car when their legs got too restless, but Evie wasn't allowed to walk around on account of the soldiers, except to go with Mama to the train's toilet. The toilet. It'd scared Margaret the first time she'd gone into that small, cramped room, locked the door behind her, and raised the lid of the toilet seat to see gravel and wooden railroad ties rush dizzily beneath her. She'd slammed it right back down, vowing she'd never sit on it. What if she fell through? Yet four days was a long time, so she'd become used to it. Gritty, black soot from the engine soon covered them from head to toe, and Mama gave up the battle to keep them clean.

Margaret glanced down at her bare feet to see black grime crusted beneath her toenails and quickly thrust one foot behind the other. The soles of her shoes, leather long gone and replaced by cardboard, had worn through again. Mama had promised to put new cardboard in them once they arrived in London. It didn't bother Margaret not having shoes. Back home, they went barefoot all spring, summer, and fall, so the undersides of her feet were hard as shoe leather. Maybe people in the city weren't used to bare feet. She frantically tried to tuck the stray ends of her hair into its plait. Evie had braided it neatly for her that very morning, but as Grandma Brown told her, *your hair has a mind all its own*.

Evie bent, trying to pick up the bread crumbs from the floor, while Timothy slapped at her hands.

"Are you showing your cousins where they'll sleep, my pets?" Uncle Harold said heartily. As he went past, he gently patted Margaret on the head and winked, then scooped up Timothy and put him on his shoulders. "I'll take care of this young fellow. You ladies go on."

Margaret followed Evie's stiff back up the stairs. Obviously she, too, felt embarrassed by Aunt Dorothy's comments. Even Mary had red in her cheeks. Only Pauline seemed unconcerned, wrapped in her air of superiority.

"And this is our bedroom," Pauline said, flinging a door wide to show a large room with two beds and a dresser. She pointed to one of the beds. "That's where you two will sleep. Mary and I will sleep in the other. We usually have our own beds, but Mother said we had to share while you were here."

"Evie and I always sleep together," Margaret told her.

Pauline bounced on her bed. "You're awfully fat, aren't you? I bet you don't leave much room for your sister."

"I take after my grandmother Brown's people," Margaret told her and headed for the window. "They were farmers and so am I."

"Margaret is big-boned, not fat," Evie added, her voice sharp. "George is going to be the same when he gets older."

Margaret looked at her sister with surprise. She distinctly remembered Evie rolling her to one side of the bed just last week, complaining that Margaret took more than her share of the bed. She struggled to push the window up and leaned out. She needed air; the house was suffocating her. After a few gulps she took a moment to look around, awed by the brilliant crimson of the tree in the front yard, one of a long line of maples stretching down the dirt street.

She'd never seen so many trees in her life as she had the last few days from the train window—or colourful leaves. Crossing from Manitoba, she'd been amazed by the number of small, blue lakes, but nothing had prepared her for the vast grey waters of Lake Superior. Even thinking of the cold, dark-looking lake now sent a chill up her spine. Dad had said their trip was better than any geography lesson at school.

She'd had to force her trembling legs to climb from the station platform up the iron steps into the stomach of the hissing monster, clouds of white steam rising from its body to envelope the waiting people. Her stomach hadn't much liked jouncing around in the train, and Timothy and Taylor's constant fretting had put her teeth on edge. But every day brought something new to see out the window, and it had been cosy wrapping herself in her quilt, snuggling up to Dad's shoulder and listening to the rhythmic *clack-clack* of the train's wheels beneath them until she'd drifted into sleep. There certainly hadn't been any cousins in matching dresses.

"Margaret," Evie called. "We should help Dad unpack and get our things."

Turning from the window, Margaret studied the room. It was pretty, she had to admit, with red rosebud wallpaper and matching white spreads on the beds. She felt a lump rise in her throat and blinked rapidly several times. No matter how pretty it was, she wanted her own bedroom at home in Saskatchewan. Wanted to look out the window and see the cow and the chickens scratching in the yard, not a house so close to the next one that she could reach out her hand and touch its brick. She'd never get used to so many buildings crowding each other. Margaret staggered slightly. It'd been half a day on land, yet her feet believed they were still on the moving train. Miserable, she followed Evie down the stairs, then grabbed her sister's arm.

"I want to go home," she said in a small voice.

"Well, we can't," Evie told her. "This is where we live now."

"Don't you want to be back home?"

Evie shrugged. "As long as I can go to school and still be a teacher, it doesn't matter where I live. Now hurry along. Dad's waiting."

Cartons and satchels surrounded the cupboard on the front lawn.

That was Evie, Margaret thought, always practical.

Uncle Harold eyed the tall corner cabinet. "I'm not sure where to put that. It won't fit in the house. We could store it in the cellar, I suppose."

Aunt Dorothy looked up and down the street. "Just put it somewhere quickly, Harold. The neighbours are watching."

"It has to be dry," Margaret's mother insisted. "I don't want damp to get into it. Martin made it for me."

Margaret caught the fleeting smile that passed between her mother and father and suddenly felt lighter. Lately, Mama and Dad had exchanged harsh words or sat inside long silences, but this look was warm and familiar, one she'd often caught between her parents in better times.

"The cellar's fine, Harold. We'll wrap blankets around it. That'll keep it dry," Margaret's father said. He began to tug at the cupboard.

"Here, let me help you with that, Martin. Mind your back." Uncle Harold hurried forward.

"You're in your church clothes," Mama protested.

"No, No. These are my work clothes," Uncle Harold told her.

Margaret gaped. Dad and most of the rest of the men in Saskatchewan wore overalls or old pants and suspenders, except Mr. Murphy who had his uniform, but she'd never seen anyone working in their Sunday tweed suit and shirt collar and tie, yet it seemed her uncle did every day at the store.

Aunt Dorothy and Margaret's mother went into the kitchen while everyone else carried the cupboard through a door at the side of the house and into the dark cellar. Coal filled half the room, waiting for winter. Climbing up the stairs into sunshine, Margaret realized the front of her dress was black with coal dust. Mama wouldn't be happy about that. Outside, she grabbed a handful of grass to scrub it off, but only managed to leave long streaks of green warring with black.

"You are a complete mess," Evie exclaimed. "I was in the cellar, too, but do you see any dirt on me? I don't know what Mama will say."

Margaret didn't know either, but she knew it wouldn't be good. She sidled into the kitchen behind Evie. Her mother stood at a table, spooning beans into a bowl. Aunt Dorothy hurried from stove to sink to table, skirts swirling over the wood floor, checking the roast and slicing bread, then to the icebox for butter. She must get awful tired if she moves that fast all the time, Margaret thought. She studied her thin, tall aunt, watching her nervous hands stirring pots on the stove, then fluttering to a dish of butter.

"You girls could put these bowls out on the dining room table," Mrs. Brown said. She looked at Margaret and frowned fiercely at the girl's dress. Margaret grabbed the beans, twitched her skirt to hide the worst of the stains, and bolted out the door.

As they all sat crowded around the dining room table, Margaret stole a look from beneath lowered eyelashes at the tops of heads bowed for the blessing: Dad's wiry yellow hair like her own, Uncle Harold's pink bald spot, Mama's brown bun newly threaded with silver. She remembered another blessing that seemed years ago, followed by her father's announcement they were moving to Ontario. Saskatchewan seemed a dreamtime now.

That night, standing in front of Pauline's bedroom mirror, Margaret struggled with a comb. Even though it wasn't a Saturday night, she and Evie had to take a bath and wash their hair before Aunt Dorothy would allow them to climb under the white bedspread. Margaret muttered to herself impatiently. The more she tried to smooth the strands of hair down, the more they flew, framing her face in a halo of gold. She threw an envious look at her cousins' short hair.

"It'd just stick straight up from your head and you'd look worse," Evie advised her, reading her mind.

Margaret sighed. Evie was right. Her hair would never fall in a sleek bob.

"If you brush your hair by the light of a candle and look in a mirror," Pauline declared, "you'll see the face of your husband-to-be behind you."

"That's just nonsense," Margaret snorted, but she immediately put down her comb. She didn't want to risk being married to skinny Lyle Ashford from back home, his huge Adam's apple bobbing nervously up and down his neck every time he swallowed.

"It's true," Pauline insisted. "I once saw Peter Stevens in the mirror so I already know who I'm marrying. He's the best-looking boy in my class and his father owns the drugstore."

Margaret averted her eyes from the mirror. True, she wasn't using a candle—as Pauline had boasted three times, Uncle Harold was one of the first people in London to have hydro electricity—but just to be safe she'd comb her hair in the daytime only.

"We didn't have to go to school today because you were coming," Mary said. "Mother says we have to go back tomorrow."

"You will be in my class, Margaret," Pauline told her. "Mother says I am to take you and introduce you to the teacher."

School! Margaret climbed slowly into the bed. She rolled over next to the wall, making room for Evie. She'd almost forgotten about school. Dad had pointed it out to them when they'd driven by on the way to Uncle Harold's: a large, two-storey, brown brick building with a single tree in the dirt yard and lots of staring windows. Her stomach knotted painfully. It'd be strange not to have George and Evie in her classroom. All the grades sat together in her old school. Evie wouldn't even be in her building as she had to go to the collegiate.

She reached under her pillow and pulled out the Flying Geese quilt pattern, then leaned over and rummaged under the bed, reassuring herself that the soft bundle of scraps was still there. She'd carried that bag clutched to her chest all the way from Saskatchewan. A fat tear fell out of her eye and rolled slowly down her cheek. Feeling that bag reminded her of home. They'd left more than the farm behind. They'd left Grandma and Grandpa Brown in the church cemetery, and Edward going to war. Was he on a ship for England or still in training camp? They had no way of knowing, until a letter arrived.

"What's that you have there?" Pauline jumped on to the bed, snatching the pattern from Margaret's hand.

Enraged, Margaret fought the urge to grab it back. Mama said that they had to get along, had to keep in mind how kind it was of Uncle Harold to let them stay, and had to take care not to cause trouble.

"Oh, it's not a dress," Pauline said, and tossed it away.

Mary picked the pattern up. "A quilt. It's very pretty," she said. "Are you going to make it?"

Margaret shrugged and plucked the pattern from Mary's hand, thrusting it under her pillow. She didn't know if she could make it. She'd been piecing simple patches since she was five, Grandma Brown using them in their everyday quilts. But the special quilts that took time and skill, those her grandmother had pieced herself. Had she learned enough about quilting from her grandmother and the other women to make one of her own? Margaret thought of the quilting bees, the women inside, the older children out in the yard running wild until one of the ladies would holler that they needed needles threaded. *We need your young eyes, Grandgirl.* She'd thread a bunch of needles, then watch the women stitch until called back outside to play. Margaret lay down and faced the rose bud wall. Somehow, Pauline had trampled on those memories by touching her pattern.

Chapter 4

"But, Mama," Margaret protested. "I could stay home and help you with the wash instead of Evie."

Her mother was sorting a mound of dirty laundry. Margaret hated wash day, hated her hands red and soft from the water, hated hauling basket after basket of soggy clothes to peg on the line, but if it kept her out of classes one more day . . .

"No. You're going to school."

"But I don't even like school and Evie does," Margaret objected.

"I know you don't," her mother replied. "That's why you're going and Evie's staying home to help me with the wash." She held up a pair of George's knickers and shook her head disgustedly as she put her hand through a jagged tear. "These may as well be thrown out. They certainly can't be patched anymore." She glanced at Margaret, then sighed and put an arm around the girl's shoulders and squeezed briefly. "I know it's a new school, but putting off going for another day won't make it any easier for you tomorrow. By tonight you will be home telling me all about your teacher and classmates."

Margaret leaned into her mother for a moment, finding momentary comfort before drawing away. "Don't throw out the pants," she said. "I'll put them in my ragbag."

Glumly, Margaret trailed Pauline, Mary, and George down the street. George chattered away, not the least bit worried about school or the fact the black stockings stretching from his feet to his knee-length pants were more darning than sock. But then George, Margaret thought resentfully, always took it for granted people would like him, and they did. She glanced down at her feet. At least she had shoes. Evie had lent her her own so Margaret didn't have to go barefoot. Back home most of her classmates came barefoot until winter cold set in, but somehow she didn't think they would in a city school. Besides, she doubted she could face her new classmates without shoes on her feet. They arrived at the brown brick building, and Margaret read the name over the door—*Talbot Street School.*

Pauline led her inside and down a long hall smelling of lemon oil polish. Their boots echoed in the quiet building, brick walls so thick the schoolyard din was barely heard. Pauline turned into a classroom, empty except for a woman sitting at a desk in front of a blackboard. She looked up and smiled as they approached.

"Miss Simmonds," Pauline said, "this is my cousin Margaret, who's come to stay with us for a while because they're very poor and her father can't find a job."

Margaret stared dumbfounded at Pauline, feeling heat creep up her neck to her forehead.

"Well, Margaret. How very nice to meet you," Miss Simmonds said. "It's sad, but a lot of people are out of work these days. But with more young men leaving for the war, jobs will open up and your father should find employment soon. It's a shame, though, that it takes a war to build an economy. The rest of us should count our blessings." Miss Simmonds raised her eyebrows at Pauline, but the girl didn't seem to notice.

"Where did you come from?" Miss Simmonds asked.

"Saskatchewan," Margaret replied. "We have a farm there."

"What a long way. I am very happy to have you in my class."

Margaret studied the teacher and relaxed. Miss Simmonds's smile reached right up into her grey eyes. Chestnut-brown hair was parted in the middle and pulled into a soft bun on the back of her head.

"My brother, Edward, is a soldier," Margaret offered shyly.

"Is he? Well, I'll be sure to keep him in my prayers," Miss Simmonds said.

Margaret instantly felt better, for herself and Edward, who'd be kept in the teacher's prayers. School might not be too bad after all.

A handbell rang in the yard and laughter and shouts stilled. Shortly after, Margaret heard the sound of footsteps and muffled whispers, then a piano in the school's centre hall began to play and children marched silently into the classroom, first the girls, then the boys, pushing their caps into pockets. Unable to meet so many strange eyes, Margaret studied her feet, thankful again for Evie's shoes. But what, she thought with dismay, would she do tomorrow when Evie needed her shoes to go to her own school? Hopefully Mama would put new cardboard in her old ones. Mulling over that problem, she didn't hear Miss Simmonds tell her to take a seat until the teacher repeated her request. Ears burning, Margaret slid into her desk next to Pauline. After a few minutes, she darted a quick glance around the classroom and peered over her shoulder to the back seats to see a brown-haired boy grinning back at her.

"That's Peter Stevens," Pauline whispered. "I told you he was handsome."

"You can share Pauline's books today," Miss Simmonds said. "But you will have to buy your own, plus a scribbler, pencil and eraser, and a pen nib. We try to provide books to students at as low a cost as possible. Maybe you have some of these readers already."

Margaret looked at the small pile of books Pauline had pulled out of her desk and her heart sank. Dad could never afford to buy her all those supplies. At home she used Evie's old texts and readers, and George used hers. She watched carefully as Pauline shuffled through the pile looking for her spelling book, but didn't see any books like those she had used in Saskatchewan.

"Stand for the anthem, class," Miss Simmonds ordered.

Margaret scrambled from her seat and faced the pictures of Queen Mary and King George and began singing "God Save the King." Finally, something familiar from her old school.

At recess, she stood with her back against the sun-warmed brick of the school, watching the older girls gathered in groups talking and giggling while the younger ones jumped rope. She avoided Pauline and her friends, not wanting to be introduced again as the poor relation, but from the sidelong glances being sent her way, obviously Pauline was talking about her whether she was there or not.

She could see George on the boys' side already in the middle of a game of catch, throwing a ball to the boy Pauline had said was Peter. She envied George the easy way he made friends. She herself spent a long time getting to know someone and had only one best friend. If only Catherine were here now, she wouldn't feel so quite alone.

"You're new," a voice growled at her elbow.

Margaret whirled around to see a girl standing beside her. Matted red hair hung in leaf green eyes. Her clothes were poorly patched, one elbow hanging out of a torn sweater sleeve. Looking down, Margaret saw the girl's feet were bare, the new day's accumulation of dirt ground into the old. A sour smell floated from her. Margaret inched away along the wall. The girl glared at her sullenly, aware of the inspection and having failed it, yet she didn't leave.

"I just started today," Margaret mumbled, fascinated by the number of knots in the girl's hair. A comb would never go through them. They'd have to be cut out.

She jumped as a hand grabbed her upper arm and yanked her away from the wall.

"You don't talk to Jean Thurlowe," Pauline said loudly. "She's not respectable. Her father's in jail." She propelled her cousin towards the school door as a teacher came out and rang a handbell.

"What did he do?" Margaret asked, wondering if she'd spoken to a murderer's daughter.

"He's a thief. He broke the window of the pharmacy and stole some tobacco and a bar of chocolate." Pauline pushed her into line under the stone arch that said *GIRLS*.

"That doesn't seem so awful . . ." Margaret began.

"No talking in line!" A man stood in the doorway, glaring at her.

Margaret froze, lips clamped together.

"That's Mr. Riley, the principal," Pauline whispered.

Margaret didn't reply. She didn't want to get into trouble her first day. She stole a look down the line and caught Jean's eye, then quickly turned away as the piano played and they marched back into class.

At the end of the day, Margaret dragged her feet behind the others, letting their voices wash over and around her. Gold and red leaves swirled about her ankles, pushed by a cold wind that had sprung up in the late afternoon. Grey clouds veiled the sun and scented the air with damp. Rain soon, Margaret thought, feeling a butterfly flit in her stomach. Maybe a storm.

Hooves clopped on the road and Margaret turned her

head to see a horse and cart draw abreast of them. Her eyes widened at the sight of a woman's hat perched on the horse's head between its ears and black stockings pulled over its forelegs. "Who is that?" she exclaimed.

"Johnny, the rag-and-bone man," Pauline told her. "He goes around to all the houses gathering up junk that people don't want."

"Why's his horse dressed up?"

"Because he's a lunatic. Only a lunatic would be a rag-and-bone man. Mother says he should be locked up in the Hospital for the Insane on the edge of town, but Dad says he's not doing anyone harm and should be left alone."

A stone hit the side of the cart with a sharp whack, followed by a clod of dirt that thudded dully against the horse's flank. Neither horse nor man reacted.

"George! Did you do that?" Margaret was aghast.

"Of course not. They did." George pointed to a group of boys walking ahead of them.

"They could spook the horse," Margaret said.

"Nothing bothers Johnny and that horse," Pauline assured her. "Everyone throws stones or snowballs at them all the time. Crazy people don't notice things like that."

As they turned into the path leading to Uncle Harold's house, a man came out, made fat by the many layers of clothing he wore. He carried a paper shopping bag tucked under one arm and a slice of bread in the other hand. Margaret stepped behind George to let him pass. They had the occasional man like him at their farm asking for work in return for a bit of food. Mama always gave them something, even when they only had a little. She watched him make his way down the road before she continued into the backyard.

Sheets snapped on the clothesline as the wind caught them. Evie was feeling each to see if it was dry enough to unpeg.

"You could help me bring these in before it rains," Evie called.

Margaret nodded and ran inside to drop off her bag. The kitchen felt warm and moist from the large wash but felt like something else, too—an argument. An argument not finished.

Her mother pulled the final shirt from the rinse tub and poked it through Aunt Dorothy's wringer on the washing machine while she turned the handle. "George," she ordered. "You can empty this rinse water over the garden."

Margaret could hear the anger in her clipped words. Mama was very mad. Something the twins did? She looked at Aunt Dorothy standing at the sink, back straight and forbidding, carrot peel flying furiously in long strips. No, not the twins, she decided.

She hurried out to help Evie, not wanting to stay in the kitchen any longer than necessary. You never knew where Mama's anger would turn next. A few minutes later the piano tinkled as Pauline practised her lessons. Margaret grinned at her sister as she heard her cousin's fingers fumble. Still, it would be nice to be able to play the piano, even if you hit the wrong notes most of the time.

They had to sit at the dining room table again for supper in order for them all to fit, even though Mama had fed the twins early and put them to bed. Aunt Dorothy sighed as she carried in a platter of chicken. Margaret and Evie had both helped prepare supper while Mary and Pauline did their piano lessons, but even that didn't help. Aunt Dorothy acted terribly put upon.

"Mama and Aunt Dorothy had a dreadful fight," Evie had whispered as they'd folded sheets, but Mary had come out and she couldn't say anymore.

Margaret looked at the faces around the table: Mama's white and strained, Dad's tired from his day looking for work, Aunt Dorothy's tight with anger, and Uncle Harold's puzzled, but trying hard to be cheerful.

As Margaret helped herself to a slice of bread, Aunt Dorothy cleared her throat.

"A tramp came around today looking for a handout," she began. "Olivia took it upon herself to give him a slice of bread and butter. My bread and butter."

Margaret placed the bread carefully beside her plate, watching as Mama's face changed from white to red.

"I will allow, Dorothy, that it was your bread and butter. I helped a man more unfortunate than myself. A little kindness and charity never hurt anyone."

"I already have charity cases right here," Aunt Dorothy said.

"Dot," Uncle Harold rebuked sharply.

"It's true," Aunt Dorothy insisted. "Look at the amount of food they eat!"

Mama's chair went over with a bang as she sprang to her feet. "I am sorry, Dot, if we are such a burden to you. As soon as Martin finds work, we will repay you for the food we have eaten."

"Now, Olivia . . ." Uncle Harold began.

Tears ran down Mrs. Brown's cheeks. "Harold, I am sorry to have spoiled your dinner. I'll just excuse myself." She ran upstairs.

Margaret's father pushed his chair back. "I'll see to her. She's not feeling well these days with the new baby coming and all." He followed her out of the room.

"Another mouth," Aunt Dorothy muttered.

"Enough!" Uncle Harold thundered.

Aunt Dorothy glared at him, stood up, and took her plate to the kitchen.

"For heaven's sake!" Uncle Harold exclaimed. He threw down his fork and stamped into the front porch. Margaret heard the squeak of a chair as he sat down. A few minutes later the smell of pipe smoke floated back into the dining room.

She looked at the food in front of her. Aunt Dorothy's food. She didn't feel like eating it now. She saw a tear tremble on the tip of Evie's nose before dropping on to her plate. Mary pushed her carrots around with her fork, while Pauline glared at everyone. George continued shoving food into his mouth.

"How can you eat?" Margaret asked him.

"I pretend nothing's happening," he said. He reached for another slice of bread. "I pretend like that all the time."

Margaret studied him curiously. How long could someone pretend? Maybe he wasn't so easygoing after all.

Evie washed the supper dishes while Margaret dried. Pauline and Mary sat at the table, school books open in front of them. That reminded Margaret that she had to ask Dad for money to buy school supplies. Probably Evie would need some, too.

Uncle Harold came through and stopped short, staring at the four girls.

"Help your cousins with those dishes," he said to Pauline and Mary.

"We have homework . . ." Pauline began.

"I said, help your cousins," he ordered. "Now!"

Pauline jumped to her feet and picked up a drying cloth. She bumped hard into Margaret as she reached for a dish. "You've ruined everything by coming here," she hissed.

Chapter 5

Finally, Saturday. Margaret felt relieved there was no school. She was running out of excuses for not having bought her scribbler or books, but there hadn't been a good time to ask Dad for money. He was always off looking for work and coming home tired and out-of-sorts. Every evening he'd sit with Uncle Harold's paper, looking through the help wanted ads until he tossed it aside in disgust, to spend the rest of the evening wrapped in a stony silence. It left her feeling bewildered not to be able to speak to her father. She'd always been able to tell him everything.

Saturday also meant she didn't have to think about Jean. The girl confused her. Every recess she wandered over to talk, even though Margaret didn't say much back. Surprisingly, though, after days of no one else speaking to her, she found herself half-watching for Jean.

Rain lashed against the bedroom window, while wind tore crimson leaves from the maple tree out front and sent them dancing through the air. For two days it had rained steadily. Water gathered in clouds passing over the great Lake Huron spilling on them, Uncle Harold had told her. Come winter, he'd added, it would turn to snow and then she'd be surprised by the huge mounds of white on London's streets. But the water was nuisance enough, lying in puddles on the roads and, unfortunately, ruining cardboard soles newly placed in her boots. Sighing, Mama had examined the soggy footwear and pronounced them no longer fit to be worn.

The morning had been spent putting the house in order, and Margaret was glad that was done. Her mother and aunt politely moving around each other had left everyone jittery.

A gust of wind rattled the panes of glass. Too wet to go out, Margaret decided, so she reached under her bed and pulled out the bag of cloth scraps and spread them over the bedroom floor in a circle around her. She loved being surrounded by colour. No matter how bad she felt, the blues, reds, and greens she fingered would lift her spirits. She had come to the decision to make the Flying Geese quilt. *In my hardest times, that's when I need something pretty, Grandgirl. Something to lighten my heart.* With anticipation she picked out the blues and light greens and put them in one pile. They would be the sky. The reds, browns, and blacks, all the darker colours, would be the geese themselves. Some of the remnants were so small, she'd have to sew them together to get a single patch, but material was scarce and she'd salvaged every bit she could find. Thank goodness Grandma Brown had been a pack rat, and thank goodness Catherine had given her the pattern. Thinking about Catherine, Margaret felt a prick of worry.

She'd hoped every day for a letter from her friend. Also one from Edward. Mama had been counting on receiving a letter from him when they arrived in London, but there'd been nothing. Were he and Christian still standing in front of their barracks or were they on a train like the soldiers who'd travelled with them? Maybe his and Catherine's letters were coming through the mail together. Her body relaxed as she fingered the smooth cotton and rough twills.

"Can I help?" Mary stood at the door.

Margaret shrugged. "Sure."

Her cousin sat cross-legged beside her and picked up a small square. "This is a beautiful blue."

"That's from my grandmother's courting dress. And this is all that's left of the sleeve of Edward's, then George's, and then, finally, Timothy's shirt." Margaret pointed to a piece of green flannel.

This pink bit is from my wedding dress—a happy day that was—and that cream is from Grandpa's shirt. First one I ever made him as his wife. This bit of white is from my first baby's nightgown, but he died shortly after he was born. All my joys and sorrows are sewn into my quilts. Margaret suddenly remembered the tiny wooden cross on a small rise at the back of the farm. The prairie constantly threatened to bury it, but Grandma, then more recently herself, forced it back, keeping the tiny grave neat and tidy. She bit her lip in horror. There was no one to keep the prairie from the grave! Well, when they went back she'd clear grass and weeds from the marker and keep it tidy again.

She turned back to the material spread on the floor. *Remembering is made up of the bad right along with the good.* She pointed to a soft brown piece. "That's Evie's and my dress we outgrew. I wore it for Sunday best until I spilled Saskatoon berry pie on it, then it became my everyday dress." She held it up for Mary to see. "Mama says I'm the messiest girl she ever saw." She'd also been wearing it the day Dad had fallen from the hay mow, but she didn't tell her cousin that.

Mary laughed. "What's Saskatoon berry pie?"

Margaret opened her mouth to answer, but Pauline burst into the room before she could say anything.

"What a mess!" she exclaimed, scattering the carefully sorted piles with a kick.

"That was mean, Pauline!" Mary said. She dropped to her knees and began to sort the colours.

"Never mind, Mary."

Margaret scooped up the scraps, crammed them back into the bag, and flung it under the bed. She didn't want Pauline anywhere near her quilt.

Glancing out the window, she saw a patch of deep blue like a promise breaking through the grey clouds. She flew down the stairs and grabbed her jacket. "I'm going out for a bit, Mama," she called, banging the door shut behind her.

It felt good to be outside after being cooped up for three days. Damp air cooled her anger-heated cheeks. She stood for a moment, looking up and down the road, deciding which way to go. Not the way she went to school, she decided, and began to walk in the opposite direction. Leaves clung slickly to the road, rain robbing them of their crunch. Her bare feet were soon white and pinched with wet and cold, but Margaret ignored the discomfort, long used to it from life on the farm. The thought ran through her head that Mama might not like her out on the city street in bare feet, but she ignored it. A horse *clopped-clopped* by doing its milk-delivery rounds. That was something she couldn't get used to in the city—the constant noise. The ringing of hooves on dirt roads, the clinking of glass bottles rattling in the milk wagon, the rumble of motor cars, the calling of the iceman. People talking and shouting at all hours. At home she heard the wind, chattering birds, the soft cluck of the chickens, and the honk of the geese.

"Margaret," a voice called from a side street.

She turned and her heart sank. Jean.

Impossibly, the girl's hair looked worse than before, plastered to her head from rain. She wore a short-sleeve cotton dress and no coat. Occasionally, she shivered as a chill swept through her.

"What're you doing?" Jean asked.

Margaret shrugged. "Nothing. Just walking around."

"Escaping Pauline?" Jean suggested slyly.

Margaret felt her lips turn up in an involuntary grin.

"I'm going to the train yard," Jean said. "Want to come?"

Margaret thought rapidly. Should she be seen with Jean, who wasn't "respectable," or go home? She thought of the house, anger in all the rooms. "Sure," she agreed.

They walked past brick houses, crossing the street at the small grocery store on the corner. People stared at their bare feet, making Margaret splash harder in the puddles. As they neared the train tracks, the houses slowly changed from brick to wood, the yards became smaller, the outhouses smellier, and the girls' bare feet no longer drew stares.

"Why are you going to the train yard?" Margaret asked.

"Gathering up any coal lying around the tracks," Jean replied. "Soon be winter and we're going to need heat. We can't afford to buy it. Watch for the guards, though. Most of them are pretty good about us taking it, but there's one old man, plain mean through and through. He won't let us take the coal even though it's spilled from the train and lying there going to waste."

At the main road a long column of marching men in uniform, feet and arms moving in unison, stopped them from crossing. Margaret felt a surge of excitement as she eagerly searched the khaki-clad men's faces. Maybe Edward was there. But then she chided herself—he'd tell them if he was coming to London. She shouldn't get her hopes up so easily. "Where are they going?" she asked.

"They're soldiers from Carling Heights," Jean told her. "That's over at the east edge of the city. They march into the country and back nearly every day for military exercises."

"My brother Edward is training to be a soldier in Saskatchewan," Margaret told her. "Do you have a brother in the war?"

"Nope." Jean watched the column end. "Let's go."

Jean began jumping over red iron tracks, searching the ground. Margaret followed, nervously eyeing the train yard. Parallel rails stretched out in front of her, some with boxcars resting on them, others empty. She spotted a lump of black at her feet and bent down to pick it up.

Holding her skirt in front of her to form a pouch, she

dropped the coal into its folds. "What if a train comes?" she asked.

"They whistle first," Jean assured her. "Besides, you'd hear all the clatter. Keep a lookout is all."

Margaret nodded and walked along the track, bending and picking up chunks of coal. Her skirt was nearly full when she heard a shout. Looking up, she saw a man in a blue uniform running towards them, waving his arms.

"Run!" Jean yelled. "That's the mean guard."

Margaret bunched her skirt in one hand and pumped her legs hard. Cold air whistled about her thighs as she ran.

As they jumped over the last set of tracks Jean stopped, pulled a lump of coal free, and threw it in the direction of the guard. "You old fart!" she screamed.

Margaret didn't stop, passing a row of buildings that merged into a blur. Suddenly, a hand reached out and yanked her into a narrow gap between two sheds. With a shriek, she collapsed against a doorway and looked up to see Peter Stevens standing over her.

"Be quiet," he whispered. "The guard won't find you here."

Jean slipped into the alley with them and slid down a wall, laughing. Peter peered cautiously around the corner of the building.

"He didn't follow you," he said.

"That was rude what you said, Jean," Margaret gasped. Then she laughed, too. It was the most fun she'd had since moving to London—in fact, almost all year.

"You sure can run," Jean said admiringly.

"I had lots of practice back home," Margaret told her. "Though Mama says it's not very ladylike."

Neither was having her dress and petticoat pulled up almost to her thighs, the lace trim on her drawers showing, she realized with horror, and Peter watching. She quickly dumped the coal from her skirt into Jean's lap.

"You keep half," Jean told her.

"No," Margaret said. "We don't need it. Uncle Harold's got a cellar full."

"It must be hard not having your dad around. When does he get out of jail?" Peter asked.

"What do you care?" Jean replied. "Are you sure you should be talking to me? What would your friends think?"

Peter shrugged. "I talk to whoever I want to talk to."

Jean was quiet a moment. "He should be out mid-January. He got six months altogether in Police Court just for stealing a package of tobacco and chocolate."

"And the window. Your dad broke our store window," Peter interrupted. "Don't forget that."

Jean glared up at him. "*Your* dad still didn't need to call the police."

"That's what law-abiding people do," Peter retorted.

"I guess you really shouldn't steal," Margaret said weakly, trying to smooth things over. She had forgotten Peter's father owned the drugstore.

Jean shook her head. "He was crazy for a cigarette and couldn't afford the fixings." She shrugged. "Said his brain just went nuts when he saw tobacco in the drugstore and went for it. Figured at the same time he might as well get candy for us kids. Sliced his arm up real bad when he broke the glass. He'd been out of work two years. Found odd jobs here and there to keep us going. Anyway, he couldn't afford the fine and couldn't afford to replace the glass, so he went to jail. Ma's not been too well since then. She's pretty mad. She says the worst crime is he's eating in there better than we are out here. They make him do hard labour for the food, though." She looked up at Peter. "So what are you doing down here anyway? Pretty far from your house."

"Watching the trains," Peter said. "Besides, every time Dad sees me he suddenly finds a chore for me, so I make myself scarce sometimes," he added, grinning.

Wind blew down the alley, carrying with it a fresh drizzle of rain. Margaret shivered. "I better get back to Uncle Harold's," she said.

"My dad might be in jail, but at least I don't have to put up with Pauline," Jean laughed, scrambling to her feet. "Your dress is a mess, by the way."

Margaret looked down at the black blotches on her skirt. There was also, she noticed, a new rip. Mama would have her hide. Maybe she could sneak in and rinse it out and sew it before Mama noticed.

"I'll walk with you, Margaret," Peter said. "Dad's expecting me at the store to help out so I go your way."

Icy needles of water trickled down Margaret's back as she walked stiffly beside Peter. She must look a sight, she thought, wet and her clothes in tatters.

"So how do you like London?" Peter asked.

She shrugged, not sure what to say. She couldn't very well tell him she hated it, not when he lived here. She looked sideways at him from under lowered lashes. Pauline was right about one thing: he was handsome with his dark brown hair and lively eyes. Light brown they were, though it was fascinating how they turned golden when he moved his head a certain way. Not that she cared, she immediately told herself. But what he must think of her! She hunched her shoulders to make herself look smaller. She hated towering over the boys.

Peter raised a hand. "I turn down here. See you at school Monday."

She half-waved back. Wonderful. Walking with a handsome boy turned her into a perfect ninny. She'd not opened her mouth once. She could have asked him about homework or school, but her brain had just gone blank. Arriving at the house, Margaret peered in the kitchen door to find the room empty. She tiptoed in.

"You're getting mud all over the floor!" Aunt Dorothy

screeched. She stood in the doorway to the hall. Margaret hadn't seen her.

Pauline, Evie, and Mary crowded behind, and Margaret could hear her mother coming down the back steps, then she was in the kitchen.

"Get upstairs immediately and change," her mother ordered. "Then you come down and wash that floor until it shines!" Her hand clipped the side of Margaret's head, bringing tears to the girl's eyes. She blinked them away. She wouldn't cry in front of Aunt Dorothy or her cousins.

Then her mother saw her dress. "You think we have money for new clothes for you?" she demanded.

Margaret shook her head and ducked under her mother's hand as it rose again. She took the steps two at a time. The twins' faces peered round-eyed from the spindles at the top. Didn't anyone have anything better to do than stare at her?

In the girls' bedroom, Margaret slowly peeled her wet clothes off.

"Give those to me," Evie said, appearing at the bedroom door, Pauline right behind her. "I'll rinse them out. You are such a disgrace." She held up the skirt and examined the tear. "I think this can be fixed."

Pauline flopped on her bed. "I never knew anyone like you," she said. "Mother says you're not the least bit lady-like."

Margaret ignored her, rummaging around in her suitcase until she found an old skirt and blouse. The skirt came up well above her knees, but it was all she had. She hoped Evie could get the coal stains out of her dress; otherwise, she'd have to wear the outgrown skirt to school.

"My mother was telling yours that perhaps you'd pick up a few manners from Mary and me," Pauline went on.

No wonder Mama nearly knocked her head off, Margaret thought. She'd better wash that floor quickly.

Evie carried off the soggy bundle. "After it dries, I'll bring back the skirt to see if you can mend it as you do the best sewing. You'll recall, Pauline, my mother telling yours what a fine seamstress Margaret is."

Margaret whirled around, surprised to hear Mama had been praising her and even more surprised to hear Evie repeating her.

"And a good thing it is, too, as she is always tearing something," Evie added as she left the bedroom.

Margaret screwed up her nose at the empty doorway. Trust Evie to give a compliment, then immediately take it away in that school marm voice. She went downstairs trailed by Pauline. When she came to the landing, Margaret stopped and whirled around. "Stop following me everywhere I go," she said.

"It's my house, I can go anywhere I want in it," Pauline told her.

Margaret took a step towards the girl, then her shoulders drooped as she wearily turned and headed for the kitchen. Pauline was right. It was her house. They were only guests. No, not even guests. The poor relations staying because they had no home of their own. Except they did have a home in Saskatchewan. She pictured their farm as she scooped water from the heating tank on the stove into a pail. She added the animals into her imaginings, and finally her family, as she got down on her knees and began to scrub. That's where they should be. A blast of cold, damp air swept over her and she looked up to see her father standing in the open doorway.

"Olivia," he called.

Margaret squatted back on her heels a moment, then quickly plunged the cloth into water and wiped it over the floor as she heard her mother's quick steps come into the kitchen. Uncle Harold and Aunt Dorothy followed.

"I've rented us a place," her father said. "And I also got school supplies for the children, and a pair of boots . . ." He smiled down at her. ". . . for Margaret."

"You didn't have to do that," Uncle Harold began. "You could stay here."

"I appreciate all you and Dorothy have done, Harold," Margaret's father said. "But it's hard on both families living like this. We'll be better off in our own place. It's not much. A small furnished cottage behind a larger house an elderly lady lives in—a Mrs. Ferguson."

"Mrs. Ferguson? Over on Talbot Street?" Uncle Harold asked.

"That's the one."

"She's a mean, old skinflint," Uncle Harold said.

"Harold!" Aunt Dorothy exclaimed.

"Always in the store trying to stretch her penny," he went on. "Trust her to rent out that leaky old cottage for extra cash. Especially when she has that huge house with only herself rattling around in it. Still, I don't like the idea of you leaving, especially with no job. Are you sure about this?"

"We'll manage," Mr. Brown said firmly.

Chapter 6

"You're not a drinking man." The woman stood in the doorway of the cottage glaring at Margaret's father. "I don't hold with a man who drinks."

"No—" Mr. Brown began.

"You have to keep these youngsters quiet," Mrs. Ferguson continued to rant. She pointed at Timothy and Taylor. "I don't hold with children who are noisy."

"They're well behaved," Margaret's mother assured her. "They won't trouble you at all."

Margaret studied the elderly woman clad in black from her high button boots to the feathered hat on her head. Perhaps she had just returned from a funeral. Thin and angular, the woman held herself ramrod straight. She was all pointy ends. Sharp elbows, a long nose like a beak, and skinny fingers that stabbed at Mr. Brown as she spoke. Margaret hated her already, and she could tell from the sudden flaring in Mama's eyes that Mama didn't much like Mrs. Ferguson either.

And Mama didn't much like the vine-covered cottage in front of them, Margaret guessed. At one time it might have been pretty, but now tightly woven mats of green spread menacingly over the brick and windows, as if poised to swallow the cottage whole. A couple of shingles lay at their feet, blown from the roof.

A black-gloved hand tentatively held out a key. "Very well then . . ."

Margaret's father reached for it, but was left groping at air as the key was suddenly pulled back.

"You're church-going people? I don't hold with people who don't go to church."

"You know me, Mrs. Ferguson," Uncle Harold said heartily. "From the department store. This is my sister and her family. I'm helping them move."

The woman squinted at him. "The department store," she sniffed. "Thieves, the lot of you."

"We are Christian," Mrs. Brown said mildly, though Margaret heard the slight emphasis on *we*.

"Well . . . in that case . . ." The arm slowly extended forward again.

Margaret's father quickly grabbed the key, struggled to fit it in the lock, then stepped back as the door swung open. They crowded forward to see their new home.

Smelly and dark! That was Margaret's first impression. A rustle and sudden scurrying brought a squeal from Evie.

"I left a candle here . . ." Mr. Brown stumbled into the room, feeling along a window ledge. "Aha."

Weak yellow light from the candle showed them the main room, but didn't have the strength to reach into its dark corners.

"A couple of lamps will brighten things up," he said.

He put the candle on a small wooden table in the centre of the room. Four chairs were set around it, one with its ladders broken. A squat black stove leaned against one wall, a pipe extending from it through the ceiling to upstairs. An ice box was fitted beneath a counter that ran along one wall. Cupboards hung above, doors askew. Margaret's father pointed at them. "I'll soon set those right," he said, pointing at the cupboards. "And the chair. Also those shingles. George can help me with them. The stove's for cooking and heat. I'll get some wood first thing Monday."

"Will it keep us warm enough?" Margaret's mother asked.

"Winters don't get as cold here as in Saskatchewan," Uncle Harold assured her.

Mrs. Brown nodded her head, but continued to look doubtfully around the room. She hadn't, Margaret noticed, taken off her hat.

"The pump's right outside the door, so that's handy," her father said.

"There's not an indoor pump?" Margaret's mother exclaimed. "We have to haul water?"

"Afraid so . . . but it's not far. George can take on that job. Outhouse behind." He stopped a moment, at a loss for anything more to say, then went on. "There's a loft up those stairs for George and the girls to sleep in and we're over here with the twins." He pointed to a room off the kitchen.

Mrs. Brown looked dubiously at the narrow staircase clinging to the wall. "Are you sure those steps are safe?"

"It's fine," Margaret's father assured her. "I'll put up a railing on the open side, but until I do we'll have to keep an eye that the twins don't go up and fall. Well, let's start unloading and get settled in our new house." He rubbed his hands together, pretending a cheeriness Margaret knew he did not feel—no one could feel looking at the dingy cottage.

Margaret wandered into a room to the right of the kitchen. The good room she guessed it would be, but it was damp and musty and she imagined it would be closed off most of the winter. She crossed back through the kitchen area into a room opposite, Mama and Dad's bedroom. A large bed stood in the middle. Margaret sat down on it, the thin mattress hard beneath her. Still daylight, yet she could barely see through the gloom caused by the curtain of vines. The windows were also coated with grime and cobwebs, adding to the dreariness. A melancholy house, Margaret decided, and she wasn't sure if her family could make it any better.

"Margaret, you can empty the ash from the stove. And keep an eye on Timothy and Taylor," Mama called.

"Can't I help Dad unload?" Margaret complained. She hated cleaning ash, always coming away grey and dusty. Ash got up your nose and in your throat.

"No, the stove needs to be done first. George, you look around outside for some fallen branches—I want to start a fire to get rid of some of this damp if I can. Then bring in a pail of water and put it on the stove to heat. Evie, we'll start cleaning upstairs and make sure it's fit for you children to sleep in tonight."

Margaret scooped ash from the black stove into a lopsided pail, its handle broken. Uncle Harold, George, and Dad brought in the cupboard first from the rented wagon, set it in a corner, and went out again.

"How did your family afford this?"

Margaret jumped. She whirled around to see Mrs. Ferguson standing in front of Mama's cupboard. When you rented a place, she decided, the owner must be able to come in and out as she pleased.

"Dad made that for Mama," she told the woman. "He made most all our furniture but it was sold in the auction back in Saskatchewan."

"Hmmph." The woman bent, squinted at the roses carved on the doors, but said nothing more. Turning suddenly, she stalked out of the cottage.

Margaret ran to the doorway and watched her cross the yard with quick steps and enter the red brick house that fronted the street. It was huge, that house. Could hold her entire family and then some. Too much house for one woman, but then who would want to live with such a grouchy person?

"Old witch," Margaret said to the twins. "Gone to get her broomstick."

"Witch! Witch!" Timothy and Taylor chanted.

"Stop that!" Mrs. Brown came into the kitchen. "She might hear you. Wherever did you two learn such a word?"

Margaret quickly bent her head to the stove.

After a supper of cold chicken and bread, Mr. Brown handed Margaret a pair of boots. "These are for you," he said. "They're second-hand but there's lots of wear still in them."

Margaret pulled them on her feet and tied the laces. The ends were scuffed slightly, and they pinched a bit around the toes, but she didn't say anything. It was lovely to have her own shoes and no cardboard soles.

"You be sure to take care of those," her mother said sternly. "Knowing you, they'll be wrecked within a day."

Margaret felt stung. She hadn't even worn them yet and Mama was already seeing them in ruins.

Dad winked and smiled. Margaret grinned back. At least he didn't see them in ruins.

"Church tomorrow," Mrs. Brown said. "George, bring in water for baths." She picked up the empty plates and started towards the counter, when she suddenly stumbled. She sat down abruptly in a chair.

"Olivia." Mr. Brown jumped to his feet. "Are you ill?"

"Just felt dizzy there a moment. Tired, I guess. I did one housecleaning this morning, not expecting I'd be doing another in the afternoon."

"You sit there and rest. You shouldn't be working so hard in your condition," Margaret's father said. "We'll take care of washing up. Maybe we shouldn't have moved in here so quickly."

"No," Mrs. Brown told him. "I'm glad we moved. I don't know if I could have spent another night . . ." She stopped abruptly and looked around at the children. "We needed our own home."

"Forget the baths," said Mr. Brown. "The Lord won't mind if we come to church dirty for once. "

"Martin, what will people say?"

"They shouldn't say anything, especially in church. But if

they want to look behind our ears, let them. The Lord knows we're clean inside. We've worked hard today and could do with the rest. In fact . . ." He reached into his pocket and pulled out five nickels. "Margaret, George, take a bowl and run down to the ice cream parlour and have them fill it up," he said. "We could all do with a treat."

George whooped, grabbed the coins, and ran out the door.

"Martin, that's just a waste of good money," Mrs. Brown protested. "I could get two quarts of milk with that money!"

Margaret stopped in the doorway, wondering whether to follow George or not.

"Olivia, once in a while you need a treat or what's the point of it all?" Mr. Brown turned to the door. "Go on, girl, catch up to George, and mind you run home fast so it doesn't melt."

Margaret raced out of the cottage and past the big house. She thought she saw the white lace curtains over the windows twitch, but it could have been her imagination. She flew down the street after George and accidentally splashed in a puddle. She still had her new boots on, she realized. She quickly took them off, cleaned them with her skirt, then tied the laces together and slung them about her neck. She didn't want to go back with her new boots wet already. Mama would just sigh, and that always made Margaret feel worse than if she yelled. Sometimes Margaret thought she was messy because Mama expected her to be. Evie was the neat one; Edward, responsible; George, cheery; and she, Margaret, messy. The twins were too young yet to be anything. Was there any point, she wondered, trailing George into the store, in trying to be different from what people expected you to be?

"Ice cream," George said grandly, holding out the bowl. "Vanilla."

The store owner flipped open the door of the huge icebox

and scooped out mounds of creamy white. "That'll be twenty-five cents."

George searched through one pant pocket, than another. "Do you have the rest of the money, Margaret?" he asked. His eyes widened in alarm. "I can only find four nickels."

"No. Dad gave it all to you."

"I've lost it," George cried.

Margaret plunged her hand down into his pocket. "You have a hole in here. It must have fallen out!"

"I found this outside the store," a voice behind them said.

Margaret and George turned around to see Jean, holding out a coin.

George snatched it out of her hand. "That's mine," he said.

He handed it to the clerk and picked up the full bowl. "Come on, Margaret, before this melts."

"You go on, George. I'll catch up," Margaret told him.

She left the store with Jean. "Thanks very much for finding our money. Though, it might not have been ours."

"It probably was. It would be odd that you'd just lost a nickel and I just found one."

Margaret nodded. She couldn't think of anything else to say, but felt there should be something.

"We moved today," she said.

"No more Pauline?"

"No more Pauline, or at least not all the time." Margaret grinned.

The sun had nearly disappeared and damp rose from the ground. Jean shivered and wrapped her arms around her body for warmth. Margaret couldn't think how to leave the girl.

"Would you like to come to our house for ice cream?" she asked, then immediately wished she hadn't. Mama wouldn't like her bringing home a girl who wasn't respectable. "If your mother isn't expecting you home," she finished, hoping Jean couldn't come.

"She's not expecting me," Jean said.

Margaret walked beside Jean, thinking furiously. What would Mama say when she saw how dirty the girl's dress and hair were? And her feet . . .

"Look at that!"

Margaret followed Jean's pointing finger into the sky. A long ribbon of black stretched out from a sinking red globe of sun towards them. The first of the ribbon passed overhead and Margaret saw it was a long line of birds, silent except for the whistle of air beaten by thousands of wings. Goosebumps rose on her arms at the eerie sight of the twisting line that seemed to have no end, then suddenly it did with only a few stray birds dotting the sky.

"Wasn't that wonderful?" Jean's eyes were shining. "I've never seen anything like that before. Usually there's big flocks of birds heading south, but never anything like that." She beamed at Margaret.

Margaret smiled back, feeling as if she'd been given a wonderful gift, one she could keep inside and bring out again and again just for the joy of remembering.

"Some day I'm going to fly just like those birds," Jean told her.

"Fly?" Margaret repeated.

"In an aeroplane. I'll be just like the birds! Can you imagine how it must feel to soar high above the ground?"

Like running fast over the prairie? "Free?" Margaret ventured.

"Yes," Jean replied excitedly. "That's exactly how it must feel. I knew you'd understand." She beamed again at Margaret, who suddenly felt warm all over.

"They use aeroplanes at the front all the time now, and as I plan to go to the war as soon as I'm old enough, maybe I'll fly in an aeroplane," Jean confided.

"Go to the war? Women can't be soldiers," Margaret said dubiously.

Jean threw her an exasperated look. "I know that. I'm going as a nurse. I'll go right to the front line and help the wounded men."

"Oh." Margaret couldn't think of anything to say to Jean's startling announcement. "Dad and I watch the geese flying over our farm in Saskatchewan every year. I'm making a Flying Geese quilt. I'll show you the pattern when we get to my house," she told Jean in a burst of generosity. Not as good as being a nurse, but it was all she had.

The big house curtains, Margaret saw, definitely did twitch this time. She held her head high and walked past, then remembered Jean was right behind her and her head came down as she went into the cottage

"Mama, Dad, this is a . . ." Margaret paused, ". . . a girl from school."

She saw her mother take in Jean from head to foot and her mouth tighten. Evie's eyes widened, but George and the twins ignored them, intent on their ice cream.

"It's nice to meet a friend of Margaret's," Dad said.

"George lost the money out of a hole in his pocket—I'll mend it tomorrow," Margaret added hurriedly. "But Jean found it and gave it back to us so I invited her here for ice cream . . ." Her voice trailed off. Mama still hadn't said a thing. This was worse than she'd imagined. There was a long silence, finally broken by her father.

"As well you should. We wouldn't be having ice cream at all if it wasn't for you, Jean. Come and sit down here. Margaret, get a dish for your friend."

Margaret crossed the kitchen and took two dishes out of the cupboard and placed one in front of Jean.

"I told Jean I'd show her my quilt pattern," she said, avoiding her mother's eyes.

She went up the stairs to the room she'd share with Evie.

Mama would tell her all about Jean later, Margaret knew, but she was beginning to think that maybe Jean was clean inside.

Chapter 7

If October was crimson leaves, golden sun, and blue sky, November was grey, Margaret thought. Slate-grey sky reflected in mud-grey puddles formed by slanting silver-grey rains. An early snowfall the day before, heavy and wet, had bent tree limbs to brush the lawn and sent her mother scurrying to find warm clothes. It had melted by noon, leaving behind a grey mist that clung thickly to the ground, trees floating above, branches hung with tear-shaped droplets. She could hear shouts from outside, where Peter Stevens and George were rough-housing with the twins. They'd be cold and wet when they came in. Margaret was glad to be at the kitchen table, sitting within the circle of warmth from the stove, working on her quilt.

She had carefully traced the flying geese pieces from the pattern—two different-sized triangles—on the back of a cardboard box, then cut them out. Beside her on the table lay her sorted fabric, in piles of light and dark. Geese and sky. Placing the cardboard template on a scrap of pale blue, she remembered prairie summer sky stretching on forever. *Quilts have a way of reminding.* She ran a pencil around the sides of the template, marking seam lines for sewing, then took up her scissors. *Cut the pieces accurately in the beginning, Grandgirl, and you'll have a good quilt in the end. Anything worth doing is worth doing well.*

Her father sat across from her at the table, folding the

newspaper in half to study the help wanted ads. Suddenly, he slapped the paper down, sending Margaret's scraps flying to the floor. She scrambled on hands and knees to pick them up.

"Every job in the paper needs experience," he exclaimed disgustedly. "Baker, toolmaker, machinist! There's nothing I can do. No one in the city wants a farmer."

"You had five days of work the week before last," Mrs. Brown reminded him.

"Picking apples so we can eat for another few days," Mr. Brown said dejectedly.

"And you got us wood for the stove," Margaret's mother reminded him.

"Yes, wood . . ."

Margaret watched him out of the corner of her eye as she began to cut triangles. Dad had picked apples at an orchard outside of town, leaving before dawn to walk the long distance, then limping home again in the dark, his face twisted in pain from his back. Mama rubbed it night after night with Sloane's liniment, though it brought him scant relief. But still, he'd worked hard and the farmer had taken a shine to him, Dad had told them, giving them a stack of wood as a sort of bonus payment for a job well done.

For those five days Dad had been busy, coming home tired and hurting, but not wearing that desperate expression he had picked up lately: mouth turned down, eyes bleak. He'd greyed, too—his skin, his hair—he'd greyed like November. It had got so she didn't want to look at him, that grey made her chest hurt. She kept her eyes on her scissors.

When she had a small stack of light and dark cotton triangles cut, she began to lay the pieces down to find which colours went best together, and after much consideration, chose two. Checking that right sides of the material faced each other, she carefully lined up their edges. Her fingers fairly itched to sew them together, to see the beginnings of her quilt. She threaded a needle.

"Margaret, you could hold this wool for me," Mrs. Brown bid her.

Suppressing a sigh, Margaret put her needle down and held her hands outstretched in front of her. Her mother looped wool unravelled from an old sweater of Edward's over them.

"I should be able to get warm vests for the twins out of this," her mother said, winding the wool into a ball. "And mittens so their socks can stay on their feet where they belong."

"I'll try McCormick Biscuits factory first thing Monday morning," Mr. Brown said. "And McClary's Manufacturing, the stove makers, after that."

"Are you sure you can do factory work with your bad back?" Margaret's mother asked anxiously. "Shouldn't you be looking at an easier job, like a clerk in an office or store?"

"I'm not cut out for store work," he told her. "I don't have fancy clothes like Harold or the fancy manner. Imagine dealing with women like that Mrs. Ferguson all day."

"I'll take a look at your good shirt later," Mrs. Brown promised. "The cuffs are frayed, but I think I can turn them once more so they'll be good as new. And I'll press your collar."

A high-pitched squeal from outside brought Margaret's mother to her feet. With the ball of wool still in her hand, she towed Margaret behind her as she hurried to the window, threw it open, and leaned out. "George, keep those boys quiet. Don't you and Peter get them all wound up. Mrs. Ferguson will be out in a minute complaining about the noise."

A moment later there was a thump at the door, then the handle turned and Mrs. Ferguson walked in, bringing a gust of cold, damp air. With an impatient click of her tongue,

Mrs. Brown quickly rushed to shut the door before their precious heat escaped.

Margaret's father slowly got up from his chair, but said nothing. You had to be careful what you said around a landlady, Margaret had soon learned, if you didn't want to be put out on the street.

"Those children are noisy," Mrs. Ferguson barked.

"They're just playing," Mrs. Brown said soothingly.

Mrs. Ferguson rummaged inside her billowing black clothes and fished out an envelope. She held it in a black-gloved hand. "A letter came to my house, for you," she said accusingly, as if incorrect mail delivery was their fault.

Margaret's mother held out her hand. "I'm very sorry about that," she said.

Mrs. Ferguson clutched the envelope tightly to her chest.

"May I have our letter?" Mrs. Brown asked after a moment.

Mrs. Ferguson slowly passed the letter over.

"It's from Edward," Margaret's mother cried.

Did Mrs. Ferguson have a letter from Catherine, too? Margaret wondered. She looked at the old woman expectantly, but Mrs. Ferguson made no move to rummage in her clothes again. Instead, her eyes darted around the room, lingering a moment on the cupboard, then to the table. Checking up on them, Margaret supposed. She hated her.

"What are you sewing, girl?"

"A quilt," Margaret said shortly. She didn't have to be polite if Mrs. Ferguson wasn't.

Her triangles were lifted from the table. Mrs. Ferguson squinted at them. "Hmmm . . ." she grunted and tossed them back down.

Margaret's father cleared his throat. "I need some wood to make railings for the stairs," he said. "Also, shingles for the roof. I noticed a leak and it could soon rot the ceiling if it's not taken care of. I'm happy to do the work if you'll provide the materials."

Mrs. Ferguson stood staring at them, mouth working as she thought. "Very well," she said and left.

"Queer sort," Mr. Brown said.

"Trying to decide if it's to her advantage to have you repairing her cottage for free," Margaret's mother said tartly.

"As long as we get the railing and shingles, I don't mind the work. Now, Olivia, what's that letter say?"

"Dear Mama, Dad, and Everyone," Mrs. Brown read. "This was dated October 24," she exclaimed. "That's three weeks ago." She shuffled the paper. *"I hope this letter finds you as well as it leaves me. By the time you get this, Christian and me will have left Saskatchewan. We are being sent to Valcartier Camp near Quebec City for training on October 30 . . ."*

"Why, he's been in Quebec and we didn't even know," Margaret's mother cried. The letter dropped from her hand.

Mr. Brown picked it up, scanned it a moment, then continued reading, *". . . and from there we'll be shipped out to England."*

Margaret's heart lurched. To England! Edward really was going to the war. Somehow she hadn't believed he'd go.

"I am sending you a money order for part of my pay for you to use, though I expect by now Dad has a new job and won't need it. I am having most of my pay sent to you and would ask that you look after it for me, though please use what you need."

"We aren't using any of his pay," Margaret's father said flatly. "We'll be fine. He'll need it when he comes back to give him a good start."

Mrs. Brown stared at him a moment, but said nothing. He continued reading.

"It seems being a soldier means mostly marching. The bugle goes at 5:30 every morning, but that's no hardship as I get to sleep an hour longer than we ever did at home. Our first parade is at 6:00 a.m. and we drill until 7:00, when we get breakfast. Then we

have a dress parade, followed by bayonet drill and musketry until noon. Being country boys, Christian and me shoot better than most. After dinner we go on a fifteen-mile route march. Twice a week we have night marches, when we go out at 8:00 and do not get back in until 2:00 in the morning! Then they make us get up at 5:30 anyway. This is supposed to make us disciplined so we follow orders, but mostly it makes us tired. You can write me at the address on the top of this letter. It will find me eventually. I miss you all, Edward.

"Well," said Mr. Brown after a moment. "At least we know he's fine. We'll write him back after supper. I'll go down to the Bank of Toronto and open an account for him. Nice to have someone in the family in need of a bank."

Margaret picked up her sewing, thinking about her gentle Edward with a bayonet in his hand. She couldn't really picture it. Edward and Dad shot rabbits and ducks and sometimes even geese, but that was for food. She couldn't imagine Edward shooting a person. Well, maybe the war would be over soon and he wouldn't go to England after all. That's what all the newspapers said anyway, and if it was written in print, well, it had to be true.

A knock on the door brought their heads up.

"If it's that old fussbudget again . . ." Mr. Brown began angrily.

He yanked the door open and Uncle Harold, Mary, and Pauline came in, arms full of packages. George and the twins pushed in behind.

"A few things from the garden Dot sent you," Uncle Harold said. "Cabbage, a squash. There's not much left now."

Aunt Dorothy was kinder from a distance, they had discovered. Margaret pulled Timothy's socks off his hands and held the small fingers in her own to warm them up. Taylor immediately pushed his hands into hers also. "Warm mine, too," he yelled. George opened the ice box and pulled out a loaf of bread and put it on the table. He cut a slice, spreading crumbs over Margaret's patches.

"You're getting my sewing dirty," she pointed out.

"Well, move it off the table."

"I was here first," Margaret told him.

"We've had a letter from Edward," Mrs. Brown said.

Uncle Harold pulled out a chair and sat at the table.

"Bread, too," Taylor hollered.

"And if these children would be quiet . . ." Margaret's mother fixed them with a stare. "I'll tell you about it."

George cut a second slice that Margaret halved and handed to Timothy and Taylor.

"Edward's at Valcartier Camp in Quebec. Then he's off to England," Mrs. Brown said.

"Being in England's no safer than being at the front." Uncle Harold shook his head worriedly. "I just read the other day that the Germans are conducting aerial attacks on the army camps in Kent."

Margaret's mother made a small noise in her throat.

"Oh, sorry, Olivia," Uncle Harold apologized. "He certainly is safer in England than at the front," he added hastily. "Things are not going well at all for our troops, I see from the *Free Press*. The war isn't going well for them at all."

"So this is your house." Pauline put her hands on her hips and looked around the room. Idly, one hand reached out and picked up one of Margaret's cardboard triangles, twirling it around.

"Put that down before you bend it," Margaret snapped. "Please," she added, catching Mama's eye.

"It's the poison gas attacks I worry about," Mrs. Brown said. "That attack in April at Ypres. Horrible. Men blinded, skin blistered, or their lungs destroyed and the lucky ones, dead."

"Olivia," Margaret's father cautioned, looking meaningfully at the children. "They have issued gas masks to the troops now, so Edward will be fine."

"Don't tell me he'll be fine, Martin! I've heard the women talk at church. Oh, the newspaper might not be able to tell us what is really happening, but I hear. Our boys faced with barbed wire, muddy trenches, people shooting at them, and make no mistake about it, they are only boys. He'll be anything but fine," Margaret's mother said. She clicked her needles together furiously.

"This place is really quite gloomy and . . ." Pauline sniffed and wrinkled her nose. "It smells funny." She leaned over Margaret. "You smell funny, too, musty and smoky."

Margaret moved slightly away from her, anxious to hear the adults talk about the war. Edward wouldn't be gassed, would he? Not if the war was over soon, she comforted herself. He probably wouldn't leave England, even if he got that far.

"I'd go overseas if I could," Mr. Brown said. "It'd give you steady money coming in, Olivia, but with my back, instead, I'm sitting here not good for anything."

"Was that Peter Stevens I saw leaving as we came in?" Pauline asked.

"He was visiting George," Margaret told her shortly.

"Peter Stevens was visiting your brother George?" Pauline repeated incredulously.

"Yes." Margaret put in a couple more stitches. "He comes quite often. He walked me home once," she added. She felt a spurt of satisfaction at hearing Pauline's gasp. Her cousin didn't need to know that she'd looked frightful at the time, that she'd never opened her mouth, and that Peter Stevens had not noticed her again except to say hello when he was over to see George.

"Well . . . well . . ." Pauline stammered.

"Well, I don't know how you can live in this awful place," she said finally.

"Shut up!" Margaret yelled.

"Margaret!" Mrs. Brown exclaimed. "Young ladies do

not use that sort of language. You apologize to your cousin immediately."

"But she . . ."

"Now!"

"Sorry I told you to shut up," Margaret muttered. "I should have just told you to stop your yammering."

"Margaret . . ." Her mother's voice held a tight note of warning.

"Olivia," Uncle Harold said quickly. "What are you making there?"

"Sweaters for the twins," Mrs. Brown replied.

"You know," Uncle Harold told her, "I can get you some work knitting. It's terrible pay, but . . ."

"Yes," Margaret's mother said instantly.

Uncle Harold held up a hand. "Now hear me out before you decide. I know a man who supplies a store in Toronto with baby sets. Sweater, booties, whatever a set is. He doesn't pay very much."

"Tell him I'll do it."

Chapter 8

"Has anyone seen Jean Thurlowe?" Miss Simmonds asked.

Margaret glanced around the classroom, but no hands went up. Jean had not been at school for four days.

At the end of class Miss Simmonds asked Margaret to stay behind. "I see you occasionally speak to Jean," she said.

Margaret nodded.

"But you haven't seen her for a while . . ."

"No."

Two small lines of worry creased Miss Simmonds's forehead. "I hope she's well. She's always so underdressed for the weather and there is a lot of influenza around." She pulled a small pile of paper towards her. "Would your mother let you go by Jean's house and take this homework to her? I'd hate for her to get behind. Also . . ." Miss Simmonds bent down and opened the bottom drawer of her desk and took out a book. Margaret read the title upside down: *Little Women* by Louisa May Alcott. "Tell her I am lending her another book to read," Miss Simmonds continued. "Have you read it, Margaret?"

"Yes," Margaret replied. "Evie borrowed it from our teacher at our last school and read it out loud to us at home. I'll ask Mama, but I don't expect it would be a problem to take the homework to Jean."

She stood a moment, admiring the smooth chestnut waves in the teacher's hair, wishing she had hair just like that instead of her own unruly yellow mop.

"Thank you, Margaret," Miss Simmonds smiled. "Have you been to Jean's house before?"

"No."

"Then I'll draw you a map. It's not too far. And, Margaret . . ." Miss Simmonds paused as if at a loss for words. "Let me know if anything seems amiss," she finished.

Puzzled, Margaret gathered up the books and piled them in her arms and opened the heavy school doors. Why would Miss Simmonds think there was something wrong with Jean? She shifted a book edge that was poking into her stomach and hurried home. The curtains of the big house moved as Margaret ran past. Nosy old woman. She debated sticking out her tongue, but no doubt that would get back to Mama, so she pretended not to see. Pushing open the door to the cottage, she was immediately engulfed by the smell of burning wood. Mama kept the fire going all day now that the weather was colder, but the stove didn't draw well, filling the room with smoke and giving Mama and the twins coughs.

Margaret threw her books on a chair. "Mama, Miss Simmonds asked me to take some homework to Jean. She's been away for four days."

Her mother sat near the window, holding her knitting to the dim light. She didn't answer right away, squinting as she counted stitches. She wouldn't light the lamp until she absolutely had to, not wanting to waste coal oil or even a candle. Margaret hadn't seen knitting needles out of her mother's hands for two solid weeks, not since Uncle Harold had brought over a huge bag of wool. Mama knitted baby sets from dawn to late at night.

Her mother frowned. "I could use your help here—" she began.

"Miss Simmonds even drew me a map," Margaret interrupted. "So it must be important."

"I don't like you associating with that girl, but if the teacher asked . . ."

"I'll go as fast as I can," Margaret promised.

"Very well. On the way back, stop at the store and get me a half pound of sugar and a half pound of stewing beef. That's the cheapest cut. Get my purse and I'll give you some money."

"Mr. Jackson at the store says we can put our groceries on credit and pay Saturday afternoons," Evie said. She stood at the sink, washing dishes in a basin.

"Putting things on credit is only putting off paying," Mrs. Brown told her. "Buy something only when you have the cash to buy it. That way you stay out of trouble."

Margaret knew she was thinking of Dad owing on the seed and farm equipment.

Her mother took out some coins, carefully counting them before handing them to Margaret. "That ought to be enough. Make sure he trims most of the fat away from the beef, though a little doesn't hurt for flavour. Hurry now."

"I will, Mama." Margaret turned to leave then stopped abruptly, seeing movement in her parents' bedroom. Dad. What was he doing home? Usually he spent his days going to the various factories looking for a job. Doing the rounds, he called it, on the off chance there might be work. She rushed out the door.

Late-afternoon dusk was gathering in the bottom branches of the pine trees. Margaret studied the map and realized she would have to cross the river to get to Jean's house on Simcoe Street. As she passed over the bridge, a beam of sun broke through a black cloud, slanting towards the water. Margaret's feet slowed at the sight of the river transformed to liquid gold, framed by trees raising black, stark branches to the sky. A mallard rose from the rushes, seemingly drawn up by the single yellow ray. Margaret knew she should hurry, but it felt as if time had stopped. She followed the duck's flight until it vanished from view. Time flowed again with the water beneath her, and she continued on her way.

She waited for a streetcar to clatter past, then crossed the road, picking her way around muddy holes, mindful of her boots. Frame houses crouched near the road, their yards unkempt with long brown grasses and weeds. In front of one, a lone chicken scratched busily away. A train rumbled on a track nearby, setting the ground trembling beneath her feet. Carefully Margaret counted five houses from the corner as Miss Simmonds had drawn on the map and found herself in front of a grey house, blue paint peeling from the door. Margaret hesitated. It didn't look very friendly. She shifted Jean's books from arm to arm. Miss Simmonds had asked her specially and she had promised the teacher, she reminded herself.

She stepped from the road to the door and knocked softly. A baby cried within and a shrill voice yelled. A blanket covering the window moved slightly, then the door opened a crack. Jean slid out, pulled the door closed behind her, and stood looking down the street away from Margaret.

"What are you doing here?" she asked, voice sullen.

Margaret blinked at the girl's surliness, then remembered her reason for coming. "Miss Simmonds asked me to bring you your homework so you wouldn't get behind," she explained. "And she said you would like to read this book." She held up *Little Women*. "It's good. Evie read it to us."

Head still averted, Jean grabbed the books from Margaret. "Thanks," she muttered, backing towards the door.

"Are you sick?" Margaret asked. "Will you be at school tomorrow?"

"I don't know. Ma's not feeling too well. I have to stay home and watch the baby for her."

A piercing shout from within whipped both their heads around, and Margaret gasped to see a red welt running down Jean's cheek from her eye to beneath her chin.

"What happened to your face?" she cried.

Jean immediately turned away. "Nothing. I walked into something. A door."

"Oh," Margaret said. She turned to leave. "Well, maybe I'll see you tomorrow."

"Where are you going now?" Jean asked suddenly.

"I'm picking up some sugar and meat, then straight home," Margaret answered.

Jean stared at the door a moment. "I'll come with you as far as the store," she said. "Wait a moment." She went around the side of the house, pulled open a door leading into the cellar, and went down. She soon returned without the books. "Come on," she said with an anxious backwards glance at the house.

"Don't you want your coat?" Margaret asked. A few flakes of snow drifted lazily out of the sky.

Jean pulled her sweater across her chest and tucked her hands up inside the sleeves. "I don't feel the cold much," she told Margaret.

They walked in silence for a while, Jean wrapped in misery and Margaret unable to think of anything to say.

"We had a letter from my brother, Edward," she said finally. "He's in Quebec for training, then he'll be going to England soon, if he hasn't left already."

Jean nodded but said nothing.

"Mama's really worried about the gas attacks from the Germans."

Again Jean nodded.

"How many brothers and sisters do you have?" Margaret asked desperately.

"Two brothers. Jack's eleven and supposed to go to school, but he mostly doesn't. The truant man's always at our house. Richard's ten. There's my sister, Brenda, she's four. And the baby. A girl. Dad's never seen her. Ma says he doesn't deserve to see her after all the trouble he's brought us. She says she won't have Dad back in the house. Well, if he's not coming back, I'll be going away, too, as soon as I can."

"Where to?" Margaret asked.

"To be a nurse at the war. I told you that before," Jean said indignantly. "I'm going to be like Edith Cavell. You know who she is, don't you?"

Margaret shrugged. The name sounded a bit familiar, but she couldn't place it.

Jean sighed. "Edith Cavell was a British nurse in Brussels. She ran a nursing school and hospital, and she hid Allied soldiers from the Germans. But the Germans found out and she was executed just a few weeks ago! On October 12! You must have seen the posters of her put up everywhere!"

Margaret's mouth formed a shocked "O." She felt ashamed she didn't know that a nurse had been killed, but the past few months had been a blur of worry with not much time left for anything else.

They stopped on the bridge to let the rag-and-bone man's cart pass. He wore only a thin shirt open at the neck despite the cool weather. He raised his hat to the girls.

"Crazy man," Jean said.

"What's his name?" Margaret asked.

"Johnny. No one knows his last name," Jean replied.

"Where's he live?"

"You see all that stuff in the back of his cart?"

Margaret nodded.

"Well, he burrows in beneath it all and sleeps there at night, wherever he stops his cart. In the real cold the livery lets him stable his horse and sleep there."

No matter how bad things seem, there's always someone worse off, so don't feel too sorry for yourself. Margaret remembered Grandma Brown telling her that as she stitched on a quilt for a burned-out family.

They hurried across the bridge to the store. Margaret could feel Jean shivering beside her and shuddered herself when she opened the store door and a blast of warmth and yellow light spilled out to mix with the cold.

"Could I please have a half pound of stewing beef? A half pound," Margaret repeated, pointing to the slab of red beef in front of her. She wrinkled her nose at the sharp smell of fresh-cut meat. "And Mama said just a bit of fat for flavour—cut the rest off, please."

"Coming right up." Mr. Jackson smiled at her and began to chop up the meat. "You're the girl that's moved in behind Mrs. Ferguson's."

"Yes," Margaret replied.

"Your mother's been in here. Your daddy found work yet?"

Margaret didn't know what to say. Mama never liked them telling family business, but the man seemed friendly and he was cutting up their meat.

"He's hopeful," she said, repeating what she heard her mother tell people at church.

He wrapped the meat in brown paper and took it to a cash register. Margaret carefully counted her money and handed it to him.

"Now," he said. "If you two wait a moment."

He went back behind the counter and pulled out four meaty soup bones, wrapped them up, and handed a package to each girl. "That's for your dogs," he said.

"But we don't have . . ." Margaret began, but Jean tugged on her arm.

"Just come on," she said.

"Thank you," Margaret shouted as Jean pulled her through the door.

Full dark had fallen while they were inside the store. Margaret thought of Evie washing dishes and having to start dinner herself while their mother knitted. She'd need the meat to add to the stew.

"I have to go," she told Jean.

"Can you come out Saturday?" Jean asked.

"I guess so. After my chores are done."

"I'll call for you after noon," Jean said.

Margaret hurried home and burst into the cottage. She handed her mother the meat.

"What's this?" Mrs. Brown asked, holding up the soup bones.

"Mr. Jackson seems to think we have a dog," Margaret explained.

"A dog?" Margaret's father said. "Where would he get the notion we had a dog?"

"Martin, the man knows very well we don't have a dog," Mrs. Brown said. "The bones are for us to make broth. I guess he's just being kind."

"Being kind!" Mr. Brown exclaimed. His face clouded over. "Charity."

"Where's the sugar?" Margaret's mother suddenly asked.

Margaret felt her heart sink. She'd been thinking so hard about Jean and Edith Cavell and Edward she'd forgotten the sugar.

"I didn't get it," she murmured.

"Well, you can just turn around and go right back out to that store," Mr. Brown thundered. His fist hit the table, making the plates jump. "You haven't got the good sense you were born with."

Margaret stared at her father, stunned. Evie turned from the stove, and George stopped in his tracks, his arms full of wood. Timothy stuck a thumb into his mouth and wrapped his arms around Taylor. Dad seldom yelled at them, leaving that for Mama to do.

Tears smarting her eyes, Margaret shoved her arms into her coat and ran back out into the cold air. As she passed the red brick house, she stuck out her tongue.

Chapter 9

Margaret smoothed the seams of the pieced material with immense satisfaction. Finally, she had finished her first row of geese. As she studied the V-shaped patches stretching in a straight line across the kitchen table, she sighed deeply. Here was order, whereas everything else in her life was confusion. Having Dad home all the time, suspenders off his shoulders and dangling from the waist of his pants, left her feeling unsettled. Back in Saskatchewan he'd even work Sundays, arriving home from church and changing into his barn clothes.

"It's the Lord's Day," Mama would protest.

"Stock don't know it's Sunday, Olivia," he'd say.

"Just see to the animals then," Mama would tell him, knowing he'd also check the wheat and pull a few weeds from the kitchen garden. He couldn't sit still. Now it seemed he couldn't move.

She stole a quick glance at him sitting opposite her, newspaper spread on the table, fingers clenching and unclenching, unused to the idleness. Even in winter he had kept busy, mending harnesses and working with wood. That's when Margaret liked him best, when he worked with wood. He'd whistle while his fingers judged the smoothness of a board, measured and cut and planed. He felt about wood like she did about material.

At least it was quiet. Timothy and Taylor slept, and Evie

had gone to study with a new school friend, wanting to catch up on her mathematics, since their Saskatchewan school was behind the city one.

Margaret looked past her father to where her mother sat near the window, needles clicking as a tiny bonnet formed and hung from them.

"Oh, no," Mrs. Brown exclaimed. "I dropped a stitch way back. How on earth did that happen? I didn't even see it." Impatiently, she pulled the bonnet from the needles. "I'll have to redo it."

"You're ruining your eyesight knitting day and night," Margaret's father said.

"It's a bit of money coming in," Mrs. Brown said absently, carefully unravelling the wool.

"A bit of money!" Mr. Brown protested. "It's slave labour is what it is. That man should be ashamed of himself, taking advantage of people like this."

"Well, we do need money coming in," Margaret's mother said, irritation creeping into her voice. "The money from the auction won't last much longer. How on earth we'll care for the children I don't know."

Margaret's fingers stilled. Mama and Dad never discussed money in front of them. Another confusing change.

"When have I ever not taken care of you?" Mr. Brown jumped to his feet, knocking his chair over with a bang. "When have I never taken care of you?" he repeated loudly.

"I didn't say you couldn't take care of us, but the fact is you are not working so there is no money. There's no getting around that."

"We should never have left the farm," Mr. Brown said flatly.

"You never even tried to get a job in a store . . ." Mrs. Brown began angrily.

"I'm a farmer, not a salesman! Don't try making me something I'm not."

Margaret bent her head and stitched fiercely. The angrier her parents' words, the faster her fingers flew. Mama and Dad had been at odds before, but never for this long. Lately, harsh words filled the kitchen every single day. *The harder times got, the more I quilted. At times it was only my sewing that kept me going.* Grandma Brown was right. The only thing holding her together was her Flying Geese quilt.

A knock on the door silenced them.

"If it's that old busybody . . ." Margaret's father yanked open the door.

"Is Margaret in?"

Mr. Brown stood a moment, then pulled the door wider. "She's here," he said.

Jean shuffled into the kitchen and crossed to the table. She had on a man's black overcoat, shiny with wear, the hem ragged. Loose, brown boots emphasized her stick-thin legs, heels slipping in and out of them as she walked, making a resounding clunk on the floor. Her dad's clothes, Margaret guessed. Jean threw a quick glance at Margaret's mother, who stared meaningfully at the newly swept floor, then Jean's boots. Red flooded the girl's cheeks as she retreated backwards, kicking the boots off on a sheet of newspaper laid at the door.

In bare feet she crossed to the table and sat, watching Margaret stitch. One hand went out and gently stroked the finished row.

"I see them," she said softly. "I can see the geese flying. I wondered when you told me you were making a quilt how you could get geese out of material, but I see it now."

A tear-shaped drop of blood fell from her hand onto the table. "Sorry," she said and immediately wiped it up with her coat sleeve.

"Are you hurt?" Margaret asked. She grabbed Jean's hand

and gasped at the raw, oozing cracks running across her knuckles.

"The cold bothers them," Jean told her, snatching her hands back. "It looks worse than it feels."

Margaret doubted that.

"Can you come out a bit?" Jean asked.

Margaret looked at her mother, who grimaced, then wearily nodded permission. She quickly tidied her sewing and put on her coat, winding a scarf over her head and tucking the ends around her neck.

"Wait a minute." Mrs. Brown suddenly got up and went into her bedroom. She came out and handed a pair of blue mittens to Jean. "Put these on."

"I don't need them, Missus," Jean held her hands behind her back. "I just forgot mine today."

Jean's hands hadn't got in that bad shape in one day, Margaret knew, and so did her mother.

"Well, use them for today and maybe one of your brothers or sisters need a pair," Margaret's mother told her. "We have extras so I'm glad someone can make use of them."

Margaret's eyes widened. Extras? With Timothy and Taylor wearing their socks on their hands to keep them warm! Obviously, Mama had knitted those mittens after they were all in bed as a gift for Margaret or Evie for Christmas.

"As long as you're sure, Missus," Jean said. She slowly pulled the mittens on, wincing as the wool caught on the chapped skin.

Margaret looked down at her own wool-covered hands. She better make sure she took good care of these ones, because it didn't look like she'd get another pair this winter.

Cold swirled around their legs and up Margaret's coat, making her shiver, but it was better than being in that tense kitchen, no matter how warm the stove was. At least she had on flannel drawers, and a cotton corset with hose supports holding up thick wool black stockings. Jean's legs were bare. How the girl stood it, Margaret didn't know. They plowed through early December snow, which came up to their knees; two days of squalls had turned the city white. They wandered downtown, crossing Dundas Street back and forth to look at the window displays: electric lamps, women's dresses, men's shirts, children's shoes. Margaret saw an electric iron for three dollars and wished she had the money to buy it for her mother. Now that they weren't at Aunt Dorothy's, the wash was done on a ribbed scrubbing board and wrung by hand and dried on the line outside if it was fine and inside if it were not. Wrinkles were smoothed with the heavy iron heated on the stove—a long, tedious job hated by everyone. But they didn't have electricity so the store iron would be of no use anyway, she told herself.

"That's her," Jean suddenly said. She pointed to an army recruiting poster attached to a telephone pole.

Margaret crowded next to Jean to see an unsmiling, stern woman staring back at her. Above the woman's head in thick black letters was written, "*MURDERED by the Huns,*" and beneath it said, "*Miss Edith Cavell. ENLIST AND HELP STOP SUCH ATROCITIES.*"

"She's the nurse I was telling you about." Jean stared at the poster a moment longer, then tugged at Margaret's arm. "Let's go in here," she said, pulling on the heavy department store door. "They have a toyland set up downstairs and we can warm up a bit."

Margaret followed Jean into the store and downstairs to Toyland. Sleds, tricycles, and giant trucks filled one section. She stopped in front of a doll with gleaming gold ringlets framing a beautifully painted china face. She stretched a hand out to stroke the doll's hair.

"Don't touch the toys," a severe voice warned.

She jerked back her hand and looked up to see a stout

woman hovering beside her. A pin on her lapel said, "Miss Wallace."

"Are you here with your parents?" she asked sternly.

Margaret shook her head.

"Then you girls better leave. We don't allow children in here."

Not allow children in *Toyland?* Suddenly Margaret saw a familiar figure standing behind a counter of men's shirts on the far side of the store.

"That's my uncle," she told the woman.

The woman glanced at him and back at Margaret and pursed her lips. "I doubt very much . . ." she began.

Margaret grabbed Jean and walked over to the counter. "Hello, Uncle Harold," she said in a loud voice.

"Well, Margaret. What brings you here? Doing some shopping?"

Margaret looked at him, dumbfounded. Where would she get money to shop? "We're just looking, Uncle Harold."

Her uncle caught Miss Wallace's eye. He reached beneath the counter and brought out two candies, handing one to each girl. "Have a sweet, then you better run along," he said. "We're quite busy today. Tell your mother and father I'll be over to see them tomorrow after church."

Sucking on their peppermints, they wandered through the farmers' market, ogling the stacks of vegetables, then climbed the stairs to the upper floor where huge haunches of beef, turkeys, and chickens hung from the ceiling on large hooks. They crowded around a potbelly stove for a moment, holding their hands to its heat, then ran outside again, dodging the street cleaner's wagon as he stopped to scoop up horse droppings.

"Hey, Margaret!" Jean pointed to a streetcar coming towards them. "Grab on to the back and it'll slide you through the snow."

The streetcar drew near, then past them. Jean whooped,

ran, and grabbed a shiny pole at the back of the car. A second later, Margaret followed, slipping momentarily on the iron track, then managing to grip a pole opposite Jean. She spread her feet wide and let the streetcar pull her along through the snow. She turned her head briefly and saw Peter standing with a shovel in front of his father's store, mouth open, watching them. The streetcar turned down Richmond Street and Margaret heard a shout. A policeman directing traffic at the corner began to chase them.

"Let go!" Jean shrieked. "Run!"

Margaret let the pole slide from her woollen fingers, staggered at the sudden release, then followed Jean down the street. The girl suddenly stopped, whirled about, and pulled Margaret into an opening between two buildings. Breathing hard, she peered out. "He's not following anymore. Didn't he look funny slipping and sliding all over the road!"

Margaret grinned back, then remembered Peter's startled face. Obviously shocked at her behaviour. Evie would never do anything that unladylike. Margaret hoped it wouldn't get back to Mama. She felt a moment's anxiety, wondering if perhaps she shouldn't have grabbed the streetcar, then tossed her head defiantly. It had been fun. Jean made her feel daring and made her feel like she did when running across the prairie. Free. Margaret looked at the colour in Jean's cheeks, her green eyes snapping with delight—Jean understood.

They continued walking, stopping in front of the Grand Theatre to examine the posters advertising the picture show playing that afternoon, *Birth of a Nation*.

"It looks wonderful," Jean breathed. "Have you ever seen a moving picture?"

"Catherine's father took us to one once," Margaret replied. It had been a wondrous experience. Real people moving around on a screen in front of her. How they got them up there, she didn't know.

"Margaret!"

She turned, but couldn't see Jean anywhere.

"Over here!" Jean called again, and Margaret followed her voice around the corner of the theater.

A narrow alley separated the theatre from the building next door. Jean frantically beckoned her.

"They've left the door open," Jean hissed. She pushed Margaret in front of her. "We could sneak in and see the picture."

Margaret backed up into Jean. "We can't do that."

"Don't you want to see *Birth of a Nation*? The poster says it's a mighty spectacle."

"Well, yes . . ."

"So, we'll never have the five cents to see it, and it'll never be back here again."

Margaret looked at the open door. She'd love to see a moving picture, but there was barely money at home for food, let alone a picture show. Somehow Margaret found herself stepping inside the door and through a red curtain into the dimly lit interior. People milled about and she and Jean quickly joined them. Jean plopped down in a seat and pulled Margaret down beside her.

"We did it," Jean whispered.

Margaret felt the velvet plushness of the seat beneath her, the warmth of the theatre, and slowly began to relax. Suddenly a hand came down hard on her shoulder.

"You girls didn't pay," a man said. He grabbed her arm and hauled her out of her seat. "I watched you sneak in that back door." He reached over and pulled Jean up, too. As he pushed them up the aisle, Margaret saw her cousin, Pauline, come in and walk toward her, looking for a seat. Right behind her was Peter. They both stopped to watch as Margaret passed.

"I am going to call the police," the usher said. "Teach you a lesson."

Margaret saw the terror on Jean's face at the word police and knew she was thinking of her father in jail.

"We didn't mean to," Margaret stammered. "It's just we wanted to see the show and we hadn't any money . . ."

The man began to drag them up the aisle as the lights dimmed.

"Wait." A woman stood up in her seat. "These girls are with me. I was looking for them everywhere."

She turned to Jean and Margaret. "You silly girls, getting the wrong door."

Margaret heard a snap as the clasp of a purse opened and then the clink of coins. "Here is their admission."

The hand on Margaret's arm dropped away.

"As long as you're sure," the man said uncertainly.

"Of course I'm sure. Don't you think I know who I came to the theatre with?"

Mrs. Ferguson! Stunned, Margaret felt herself shoved into a seat. Jean dropped down beside her.

"Mrs. Ferguson," Margaret began.

"Be quiet. I came to see the show, not you," the woman said. "I don't hold with girls who talk all the time."

Margaret held her tongue and watched as the purple curtains swished open and the title, *BIRTH OF A NATION by D. W. Griffith,* flashed across the screen. Soon she was caught up in the saga of the Camerons and Stonemans and the horror of slavery and the American civil war. Tears streamed down her face as Elsie's world fell apart, shattered by war, and her brother lay dead on the battlefield. Would Edward be lying dead on a battlefield somewhere?

As they came out of the dim theatre, Margaret blinked, waiting for her eyes to adjust to the late afternoon light. She tugged on the coat of the woman in front of her.

"Thank you, Mrs. Ferguson," she said shyly. "It was the best show I ever saw."

"Thank you, Missus," Jean echoed.

"What do you think your parents will say about this little escapade? About your sneaking in without paying the admission? That is just like stealing," Mrs. Ferguson scolded. Not waiting for their answer, she began to stride down the street, black skirts clearing a path through the snow. Margaret and Jean hurried to keep up.

Mrs. Ferguson stopped suddenly and pointed at Jean. "You, girl! Go home."

Margaret watched as Jean scurried away, then followed in Mrs. Ferguson's wake.

Mama and Dad were going to be very angry. Mrs. Ferguson was right. It was as bad as stealing, sneaking into the pictures without paying. And they would find out. If not from Mrs. Ferguson, then from Pauline. Her cousin would make sure of that. She remembered Peter's surprised face beside Pauline's. Had they gone to the show together? He must think her horrible—hanging on to the back of a street-car and sneaking into the picture. It shouldn't matter, but somehow it did. She tucked that worry away and turned to the more important one. Mama! She would blame Jean and never let her see her friend again. Margaret stopped walking. Jean *was* her friend, her only friend in London, and she'd miss her terribly if Mama didn't allow them to be friends anymore. Catherine was still her best friend, she thought loyally, but she'd never do anything like sneak into the picture show or take coal from the railway tracks. Jean was—fun.

At the sidewalk leading to the brick house, Mrs. Ferguson stopped. "I paid your way into the pictures and now you have to pay me back."

"I don't have any money," Margaret told her.

"Well, then, you'll have to work it off." Mrs. Ferguson looked around the yard. "Every Wednesday and Saturday afternoon you are to come to my house."

"To do cleaning?" Margaret asked.

Mrs. Ferguson waved a hand at her impatiently. "I have Hilda to do that, who, no doubt, does it much better than you ever could. I mean you to keep me company. A companion—that's what you'll be. You can bring that sewing you're always working on, if you like. Tell your mother I asked for your company."

Mrs. Ferguson started up the walk, stopped, and turned. "You can tell them I took you to the pictures as payment for your companion services," she said. "I don't suppose you'd have trouble with bending truth a bit, a girl who would sneak into a theatre." She raised an eyebrow. She went a little farther and stopped again. "Can you read?"

"Yes," Margaret replied.

"That other girl, too?"

"Yes."

"Fine, you can bring her along with you."

Margaret watched the black skirts climb the big house steps, then disappear indoors. Slowly she began to walk back to the cottage, relieved that Mama and Dad need never know about what she'd done. Except—she looked back at the brick house—now she was Mrs Ferguson's companion!

Chapter 10

"Pack up your desks, class. It's time for calisthenics," Miss Simmonds ordered.

A groan went up from the pupils. Wednesday mornings, the entire school assembled outside—rain, snow, or sun— and Mr. Riley put them through a routine of exercise, though, as Jean pointed out to Margaret, he merely commanded them and didn't take part himself.

They filed outside and faced the principal. "Line up! Arms out!" Mr. Riley barked. "That is the space you should be from the person next to you at all times!"

Margaret pushed her outstretched hand against Jean's shoulder, then let it drop.

"Before we begin, I wish to bring up a matter of grave concern and that is . . ." Mr. Riley paused. "Spies. Enemy spies."

The playground fell immediately silent, intrigued.

"You may think we in Canada are immune from the dangers of war, but you would be wrong." His breath puffed white in the cold. "The very person standing next to you on the streetcar, at the market, in the store, might be a German spy."

Margaret exchanged a wide-eyed glance with Jean.

Mr. Riley cleared his throat. "We must all do our bit for the war effort and even the smallest child can watch for spies. There are certain peculiarities that give away a spy.

Odd behaviour, furtiveness, continual questions, and an awkward way with the English language. I would ask that you all be on your guard and should you see any of the above behaviours, report it to the nearest police officer."

The playground erupted into an excited buzz.

"Stride jumps!" Mr. Riley shouted. "Breathe deeply and begin."

Margaret and Jean hurried from the schoolyard at the end of the day.

"Don't forget we have to go to Mrs. Ferguson's," Margaret reminded Jean.

"What did your mother say about the moving picture?" Jean asked.

Margaret grimaced. "I told her—and Pauline—that Mrs. Ferguson took us as her guests. I guess that wasn't too much of a lie—Mrs. Ferguson did pay."

"I have to go home first to feed the baby," Jean told her. "Once she's settled I'll try to get away, but I can't promise."

"You have to come. I can't go there alone," Margaret wailed.

Jean stopped at the corner. "It depends how Ma is." She turned to go down the street, when suddenly she stepped back, clutched Margaret's arm, and pulled her behind a tree trunk. "Don't look, but there's a man there. Sitting on a stump. And he's behaving oddly."

"Where?" Margaret asked. She craned her neck to see, but Jean yanked her back.

"I said, don't look!"

"How can I tell if he's behaving oddly if I don't look?"

Jean chewed her lip a moment. "Well, take a quick peek then. Don't let him see you."

Margaret peered around the tree trunk, then ducked back. "He's writing something on a paper and he keeps looking down at the river and the bridge."

Peter and George came around the corner. Margaret

waved at them wildly, then put a finger to her mouth for quiet as she signalled for them to come behind the tree.

"What's going on?" Peter asked.

"There's a man behaving oddly," Margaret whispered. "He's acting peculiar, just like Mr. Riley said to watch for. Do you think he's a spy?"

Both Peter and George stuck their heads around the tree trunk. "What do you think he's doing?" Peter asked.

"I'll walk by him and see," George announced.

"What if he grabs you and takes you away?" Margaret protested.

"Well, you can run home and tell Dad to rescue me."

They watched as George casually walked down the road, slowing his steps as he passed the man. At the end of the block, he turned and ran back. The man glanced up as George passed and smiled.

"He's got a nice face," Margaret said.

"Most spies do," Peter told her. "That way no one suspects they're spies."

George ducked behind the tree. "He's drawing a map of the river," he announced. "He must be a spy."

Peter's eyes bulged out of his head. "I have to go help out at the store. I'll tell my dad and he can phone the police."

"I bet we'll get a reward or medal for turning him in," George told them excitedly.

"That's all very fine, but we have to get home, and we have to pass right by him to get there." Margaret peeked around the tree trunk, then pulled her head in quickly. The man had been staring at them!

"We'll all go together," Jean said. "He wouldn't hurt all of us."

Huddled in a group, they stiffly walked past the man. Margaret stole a look from the corner of her eye. The man smiled back at her, and she quickly averted her eyes, prodding

George to hurry. Once past, they broke into a run and went off in separate directions.

"Don't forget to call the police, Peter," George called.

He and Margaret ran towards home, catching up to Evie as they arrived at the door to the cottage. "Evie," George stopped for breath.

Margaret immediately took over relishing the news. "We saw a German spy!"

"I was going to tell her," George protested.

"You were taking too long."

"A spy? Are you sure? Where did you see him?" Evie asked.

"Sitting on a stump, drawing a map of the river," George told her.

Evie took off her coat and set her books on the table. "And why would the Germans want a map of the Thames River? You two have the biggest imaginations . . ."

"It wasn't our imagination," Margaret interrupted. "We really saw him."

"I'm sure you saw someone and then jumped to conclusions," Evie said calmly.

"You're just mad because you didn't catch a spy," Margaret rounded on her sister.

"Well, you should have gone and asked him if he was a spy, then you would have known for sure," Evie said.

Margaret bridled at the amusement in her sister's voice. "That's just like you, Evie. Spoiling everything."

"You know you have your coat buttoned up all wrong," Evie told her.

"If you two could stop fighting," Mrs. Brown said, "I could do with some help hanging this washing. George, you can carry out that basket. Evie, there's the twins' overalls in the tub to be scrubbed and that's the last of it. Margaret . . ."

"I have to go to Mrs. Ferguson's today. I'm expected,"

Margaret reminded her, feeling a moment of triumph. Evie would have to help Mama with the laundry all on her own. Mrs. Brown raised her eyebrows at her, then sighed. "Go on, then."

Mama and Dad had thought it very queer, indeed, that Mrs. Ferguson had taken Margaret to the picture show and queerer still that the woman wanted Margaret to visit her. Mama had given her a look that said she knew there was more to it than Margaret was telling them.

"You don't have to go," Dad had said. "She might be our landlady but she doesn't own us."

"I don't mind," Margaret had replied, fibbing miserably.

At the back door of the red-brick house, Margaret clutched her bag of scraps and wished fervently that Jean were with her. She looked back at the cottage. Mama stooped, pulled a pair of pants from the basket, and pegged them to the line, then paused, placing a hand on her back. She did that a lot lately, Margaret realized. The coming baby obviously tiring her mother.

She knocked softly on the door. Maybe Mrs. Ferguson wouldn't hear, then she could say she had tried to visit only to find no one was at home, but the door swung open. Hilda, Mrs. Ferguson's maid, gestured for Margaret to come in, then disappeared down a hall. Margaret stood alone in an agony of indecision. Was Hilda coming back? Should she have followed the woman? Should she try to find Mrs. Ferguson herself or stay at the back door? Finally, Hilda returned and beckoned to Margaret to follow her. At a closed door she stopped, rapped, then whirled about, and vanished again.

Left alone, Margaret gulped hard. The hall was panelled in dark wood that swallowed any daylight that dared find its way in. The air smelled old and stale, like a tomb, she thought. Quiet as a tomb also. She could hear every thump her heart made. She gave a little shiver and pulled her bag more tightly to her chest and leaned an ear against the door.

Maybe Mrs. Ferguson was dead in there! Maybe that's why Hilda didn't say anything. She wanted Margaret to find the body.

"Are you going to stand outside that door all afternoon or come in?" a voice shouted from inside.

Margaret breathed a sigh of relief. Mrs. Ferguson wasn't dead. She turned the handle and went into the room.

Darkness dominated this room also—sombre furniture, drab papered walls, thick brown rugs. Mrs. Ferguson, dressed in black crepe, was a shadow seated in front of a small fire. Watery sunshine filtered through thin muslin curtains covering tall windows, pushing back some of the gloom.

"Where's that other girl?"

"Jean will be here soon," Margaret said nervously.

"Well, don't just stand there." The old woman waved her hand towards a chair opposite her. "Sit down."

Margaret slowly unbuttoned her coat and walked over to the chair. Once seated, she studied the room further. A piano stood in the far corner, ivory keys covered and no music in sight. Behind it, shelves stuffed with books stretched from floor to ceiling. Margaret's eyes roamed the room, coming to rest on a picture on the fireplace mantel of a young man in uniform.

"That's my son Blair," Mrs. Ferguson said, seeing her interest. Her voice softened. "My eldest. Bright, cheerful, handsome. Didn't the girls flock around him. He was killed in April at Ypres." Her voice became brisk.

"I'm sorry," Margaret said. So that was why Mrs. Ferguson dressed in black; she was in mourning. "My brother Edward is going to the war soon."

"I didn't know you had an older brother. So he's doing his bit for the war, is he? Well, I'm glad of that but I'm sorry for your mother. It'll be a heartbreak for her when that final telegram comes."

Margaret felt her stomach knot at the thought of Edward being hurt or—killed. What a horrid woman to say that! "The war might be over before he goes," she said.

Mrs. Ferguson merely grunted, picked up a newspaper lying on the table next to her, opened it, and proceeded to squint at the printing. As if she weren't even in the room, Margaret thought indignantly. Well, if Mrs. Ferguson could be rude, so could she. She crossed over to a table and calmly spread out her patches. Let the old woman read her newspaper; she would work on her quilt.

Suddenly the door opened and Hilda showed Jean in.

"Well, there you are. What kept you?" Mrs. Ferguson asked.

"I had to go home first," Jean said. She gently eased her coat off her shoulders, then cradled her right arm with her left hand.

"Can you read?" Mrs. Ferguson asked.

"Yes," Jean said.

"Well, pick out a book and read to us or you can read from the Bible if you prefer." Mrs. Ferguson turned a page and buried herself behind the newspaper.

Jean raised her eyebrows at Margaret, then crossed to the bookshelves. "These all yours, Missus?"

"Most of them were my dead husband's."

Jean tilted her head to read the titles. "I don't have much use for the Bible, though there are some interesting stories in it."

"Stories," Mrs. Ferguson exclaimed. She dropped the paper with a rustle. "Those aren't stories. They are our Lord's teachings."

"I don't care much for church and the Lord's teaching. Might be fine for other people, but not for me."

"Scandalous," Mrs. Ferguson said. "What is the world coming to? Young women not going to church, wanting to vote along with men. I've just been reading about this Mrs.

Nellie McClung coming to give a lecture at the Masonic Temple Hall. *Should Women Think?* That's what she's talking about. A suffragette, though I do see she supports the temperance movement. You probably want to be just like her."

"No," Jean said firmly. "I'm going to be a nurse like Edith Cavell. I'm going to go to the war and help the wounded men."

"Nursing! I don't hold with women going off to war. It's for men. Women aping men in dress and thinking they can take on the affairs of men. Drinking, playing billiards, betting on horse races, voting. Becoming far too mannish. A woman's place is in her own home, being subject to her husband, not strutting around at a war with men. If you want to do something useful for the war effort, join the Red Cross knitting and sewing group."

"I don't need a husband to keep me," Jean said grandly. "Neither did Edith Cavell."

Margaret studied her friend closely. It had never occurred to her that she might not marry. Didn't every woman get married? Well, except for the old spinsters that no one wanted.

"I might even have a ride in an aeroplane if I go over to the war."

"An aeroplane?" Mrs. Ferguson echoed. "Why would you want to leave God's good earth in one of those dangerous contraptions?"

"Why would I want to stay?" Jean retorted. She turned back to the bookshelves. "*Jane Eyre?*"

"Fine," Mrs. Ferguson said shortly.

Jean flopped in a chair near the fire, opened the book, and began to read. Margaret laid a blue triangle next to a brown one and began to stitch a seam. Jean read quite well, Margaret noted, not tripping over the words as many of their classmates did. Her speech took on the voice of the characters, bringing the story to life. Margaret felt herself relax, her needle going up and down through the material to the rhythm of Jean's voice.

They all jumped when the door swung open and Hilda wheeled in a tea cart and left.

"Girl," Mrs. Ferguson pointed at Jean, "you can pour."

Jean awkwardly held the teapot with her left hand and aimed an amber stream towards a cup. It missed and puddled on the tray. Margaret quickly mopped the tea up with a napkin.

"Left-handed people are always clumsy," Mrs. Ferguson said.

"I'm not left-handed," Jean said.

"Then why are you pouring with your left hand?" Mrs. Ferguson demanded.

"I . . . I walked into a door and hurt my other arm," Jean said.

Margaret looked at Jean curiously. That must have happened when she went home. She'd been fine at school earlier. Jean must be accident-prone, walking into things so much. She selected a sandwich and bit into it. Chicken. Her mouth watered. It'd been a while since she'd tasted chicken, but the sandwich was so small it was gone in two polite bites, leaving her hungry for more.

Jean scooped a handful of sandwiches onto her plate and popped one whole into her mouth.

"Don't wolf your food," Mrs. Ferguson said sternly. "Didn't your mother teach you manners?"

"No, Missus," Jean said calmly. "We don't have time for manners at my house."

"If you are a slovenly girl, you will be a slovenly woman. What man is going to want a slovenly wife?"

"I already told you I'm not ever going to be a wife," Jean said, leaning over and taking two more sandwiches. "Women are starting to work in the factories now that more of the men are gone. They drive ambulances overseas. They don't need to be wives."

"Young women should not be out taking a man's job," Mrs. Ferguson said. "They need to remember that God gave man first place in this world. A woman's job is to help a man fill with honour the place that God has given him."

"Lots of women work. Miss Simmonds is our teacher and she's a woman," Margaret told her. "And my mother works knitting baby sets for the store."

"Some men are weak and therefore women are forced from their proper roles to take on men's positions. Your mother should be knitting for the war effort, not money," Mrs. Ferguson said.

Margaret felt a rush of anger. Did Mrs. Ferguson mean her dad was weak? And yet maybe Mrs. Ferguson was right—that did seem to be the way Dad felt, too. He hated Mama working so hard, hated her bringing in money when he couldn't. She'd heard her mother telling him that in hard times everyone in a family pulled together to make ends meet, but he still minded.

Suddenly the door flew open and a man breezed into the room. Margaret's face froze, while Jean's jaw dropped open.

He grinned at the girls, sat next to the fire on a sofa, and crossed his legs. "Mother, I've just had the strangest experience. I was questioned by the police as to whether I am a German spy. It appears some children thought I was making a map of the Thames River for the Germans to use. It took some doing, but I managed to convince the police I really was an art student sketching the beautiful river in its winter glory and was home on a visit from school to see my lovely mother."

He picked up a sandwich and poured himself a cup of tea. "They will probably call around later to confirm you really are my relation. Now, who are these charming ladies?"

Margaret dared not look at Jean.

"Just two girls. You need not bother with them."

"But I have the feeling we've met before, though I can't recall where." The man put his head to one side and studied them.

Margaret swallowed hard. "I'm Margaret Brown and I live in the cottage behind the house, and this is my friend, Jean Thurlowe." She hoped he wouldn't tell his mother who'd called the police! Studying his friendly brown eyes and the generous smile lighting his thin face, she thought not.

"I'm pleased to meet both of you. I'm Allan Ferguson and I go to school in Montreal where I study art, though perhaps I should really think of being a spy instead of an artist, as I seem to suit the role better."

Mrs. Ferguson got to her feet and walked to the window. "Perhaps if you were in uniform they would not have taken you for a spy." She pulled back the curtain. "Your mother's putting out laundry again. Seems that all she does is wash. But I guess with a pack of children that's the way it is. It appears you will also soon have an addition. A bad time for that."

"Mama says it's never a bad time to have a baby," Margaret told her indignantly, feeling colour flood her face. Mrs. Ferguson should not be commenting on her family, especially Mama being in the family way, with such familiarity and certainly not in front of Allan. No one talked about the baby and Mama seldom went out these days unless well wrapped in a coat and shawl that covered the swelling of her stomach.

"Well, she'll wear out her washing machine." Mrs. Ferguson said.

"We don't have a washing machine," Margaret told her, wondering if it'd be polite to take another sandwich. They'd been so small, one wasn't very satisfactory. "We had one in Saskatchewan but couldn't bring it with us so Dad sold it. We use a scrubbing board."

"A scrubbing board!" Allan exclaimed. He joined his mother at the window.

Margaret took the opportunity to sneak a sandwich and, copying Jean, crammed the whole thing into her mouth. She saw Jean slip a couple more into the pocket of her skirt. Horrified, she realized they'd cleaned off the plate. Mama told her to never clear the plate when out in company.

"Those boys run around all day shouting and giving me a headache. I should never have rented the cottage out," Mrs. Ferguson complained. She stood at the window a moment longer.

She whirled around, eyed the empty plate, then the two girls. "Go home now. I'm tired."

Allan smiled sympathetically at the girls, then nodded his head for them to go.

Jean helped Margaret gather up her material. Mrs. Ferguson leaned her head on the back of the chair and closed her eyes. She did look tired, Margaret thought. Her face was pale, but the lips drawn down at the corners spoke more of disappointment than exhaustion. Mrs. Ferguson, Margaret decided, was disappointed by life.

As they quietly let themselves out of the room, the woman's eyes flew open. "I'll expect you Saturday afternoon. We'll go see Mrs. McClung."

Chapter 11

Margaret had often passed the Masonic Temple Hall, but she had never before gone into the imposing building. Following Mrs. Ferguson's black-clad figure between two large columns, she went through the double doors into the main hall. Allan accompanied them, despite his mother's continual comments that she could not begin to fathom why he'd bother to come hear a suffragette.

"I'm interested in what women think. After all, they make up half the world's population," Allan told her.

Margaret had one awful moment when a woman at the entrance asked for a ten-cent admission, but Mrs. Ferguson calmly pulled out her change purse and paid everyone's fee.

Squeezed between Jean and the large bulk of a strange woman, Margaret felt slightly faint from the stifling heat and the rising smell of wet wool, people's bodies, and the fumes of the coal furnace. It was largely a female audience that afternoon—Mrs. McClung had spoke at a special lecture for men the previous night. Voices rose in a deafening din, and Margaret craned her neck to see around the wildly bobbing feather in the hat of a woman in front of her. Suddenly the voices stilled as a woman took the stage.

"I am pleased to present to you Mrs. Nellie McClung, authoress and lecturer. Mrs. McClung's talk this afternoon will be touching on the war, temperance, and the vote for women. Her address is entitled: *Should Women Think?*"

Margaret moved to the edge of her chair and watched as a second woman walked to the podium, smiled out at the audience, and cleared her throat.

" 'No woman, idiot, lunatic, or criminal shall vote'—from the Election Act of the Dominion of Canada. All that stands in the way of the realization of the effort to secure legislation to provide all women with votes is prejudice. And believe me, when it comes to length of life, prejudice has any old yellow cat beaten every way."

Margaret glanced over at Mrs. Ferguson's disapproving face. This wouldn't suit her at all. Allan, she noticed, made swift, sure moments with a pencil on a sketch pad on his lap. His head swivelled from Mrs. McClung to the white paper, then back again.

"Woman was looked upon as a delicate thing to be nurtured and protected in the home. If she showed any intelligence, she was pronounced a witch and they burned her. Some men seem to think that if a woman is permitted to acquire education, she may some day not get home in time to have her husband's dinner ready. And what is more terrible than that?"

Polite laughter swept through the audience.

"When is she going to speak about temperance?" Mrs. Ferguson whispered loudly to Allan.

"And what do women think of the war?" Mrs. McClung continued. "I have watched a good many boys go away to war, but I've never heard a woman cheer when they went."

Margaret remembered the men crowding around Edward, shaking his hand and slapping his back, and her mother standing very still, watching the wagon that carried Edward away from them.

"Since the war broke out," Mrs. McClung continued, "women have done a great deal of knitting. Some have seen nothing in it but a 'fad.' It is more than that. It is the desire to help, to care for, to minister; it is the same spirit that inspires our nurses to go out . . ." Margaret glanced at Jean and saw the girl's face light up. ". . . and bind up the wounded and care for the dying. Men make wounds and women bind them up." She paused a moment. "So the women, with their hearts filled with love and sorrow, sit in their homes and knit."

Into the quiet room a sob broke from a woman's throat, quickly muffled. Mrs. Ferguson, Margaret saw, sat upright, body and face rigid, gloved hand tightly grasping her umbrella handle, as if she might break into pieces if she it let go. Margaret suddenly wished she were home, working on her quilt and not hearing that war hurt people so much. Her stomach began to feel queasy. The war would be over before Edward went, she kept repeating to herself, but the assurance wasn't working. Mrs. Ferguson had lost her son.

The room reeled about her as Mrs. McClung told the audience that every time she saw a soldier drunk she felt like apologizing because they had exposed him to temptation on his weak side and that she was working on a temperance campaign. Mrs. Ferguson nodded her head in satisfied agreement.

The woman in front of Margaret suddenly threw a fur stole over her shoulder and the head of a dead fox flopped across her back, lifeless eyes peering at Margaret. Black dots crowded her sight, as she stared at the head in horror.

"Come outside. The fresh air will help."

Allan's face swam in front of Margaret as he helped her from her seat. They threaded their way through the people standing at the back of the hall and into the cold outdoors. Margaret took deep breaths and felt her head clear.

"I'm sorry," she said. "I made you miss the rest of Mrs. McClung's talk."

"I don't think she has much left to say," Allan assured her.

"It was just so hot in there and she was talking about the

war and the soldiers . . . and then that fox . . ." Margaret shuddered.

Allan leaned back against one of the columns. "Your brother Edward enlisted, Mother says."

Margaret nodded miserably. "I didn't like Mrs. McClung talking about the wounded and dying."

Allan said nothing for a long moment, then spoke haltingly. "I want to say he'll be fine, but that wouldn't be true because there is no guarantee he will be fine. My brother, Blair, is not coming back. And if Edward comes back alive, should this war ever end, he probably will not be fine even then. He'll be different from the Edward you knew."

"He already is," Margaret told him tearfully. "As soon as I saw him in his uniform I knew he was different. I don't let Mama or Dad see, but I check the casualty lists in the newspaper; the shocked, wounded, seriously ill . . ." She paused. ". . .then the killed, to see if his name is there. I don't want to, but I can't help looking."

"There's not quite the feverish patriotism in Montreal that you see here. A lot of people there are not in favour of the war," Allan told her. "At the beginning everyone was running to join up, thinking it'd be over soon—a few months and they all wanted their chance to go to war to join in the glory. Maybe have a break from their everyday lives. Now we know it has turned into an ugly man-eating war, yet people here can't understand why I'm not rushing to join up. They think I should still do my duty. While I don't agree with Mrs. McClung on all her views, she is right about women and war. When I waited for my train in Montreal I watched a regiment pull out. The women stood silently on the platform. The men waved wildly and talked boisterously, but the women . . . It hurt me to watch them."

From inside the Masonic Temple Hall, a man began to sing. Allan turned bleak eyes on Margaret. "The truth is I don't want to die and if I go overseas, I probably shall. It's not because I'm scared of death, but there's so much I want to see and do with my life, so much beauty in the world, that I don't want to throw it away on a stupid war." He suddenly smiled. "I imagine I'm boring you dreadfully."

Margaret shook her head. Everything he said was so different from what they were usually told. "At church, the minister said that we had to stop the German horror and that every able-bodied man should go and every woman should encourage their husbands, brothers, sons, and fiancées to go despite the hardship of having them leave. He said they had to make the final sacrifice if necessary. And Mr. Riley—he's the principal at my school—he said when King and Country call, every boy and girl, man and woman, has to do their part to help win the war. That's why we thought you were a spy. He told us to watch for them, what they looked like. Don't you want to help win the war?"

Allan thought a moment. "Yes. The war is an abomination and the Germans have to be stopped. I never told Mother, but during a stopover in Toronto I got off the train to stretch my legs and a woman dumped white flour on me."

"Why?" Margaret asked.

"It's a sign I'm a coward. They see a young man out of uniform and they think him a coward." He stared off into the distance, looking miserable. "And perhaps I am. Am I a coward, Margaret Brown, for wanting my life?"

He didn't wait for her reply. "Mother says she wants me to join up like Blair did." He winced slightly when he said his brother's name, but his voice remained mild. "Blair was always her favourite. He was easy to understand, whereas I confused and angered her. Imagine wanting to spend your life immersed in colour and form and shape. Actually, you, Margaret, might understand how I feel. I saw your sewing spread out on the table at Mother's. You have an eye for contrast and colour."

The best lessons in colour, Grandgirl, are in the land around you, blue prairie sky, golden fields, green pastureland. See how God coloured his world and follow his example.

How would she feel if she were going to war, knowing she might not see Saskatchewan again? Edward had been excited to be leaving, but she would miss home. She tore her mind from the prairie to listen to Allan.

"Mother says she wants me to join up, yet I think another part of her is desperately hoping I don't. People speak of the war as being overseas, but it is here at home too. So much pain and sorrow for those left behind."

People trickled from the hall, then the flow increased as the lecture ended.

"Don't mind Mother," Allan said hurriedly, beneath the noise of the crowd. "She's grieving in the worst way for Blair and trying hard to keep a stiff upper lip, which has the effect of making her tongue extra sharp. You and Jean are good for her. Promise me you won't desert her. She'll need you all the more now."

Startled, Margaret watched him greet his mother. Why would Mrs. Ferguson need Jean and her?

"Now I," Allan said grandly, "will treat you ladies to the chicken salad tea at Smallman and Ingram's Department Store."

Mrs. Ferguson opened her mouth to protest, but Allan jumped in. "Now Mother, it is only fifteen cents a person, a very reasonable price, and I do have a bit of money. Believe it or not I have managed to sell some of my scribblings."

He herded them downtown and into the large department store. She should have been delighted, Margaret knew, with wrought-iron chairs, the bright lights and warmth, the Christmas tinsel and greenery, and the delicate china teacups. Evie would give anything to be in her place, but she couldn't feel happy. Her head ached with thoughts that churned ceaselessly: Edward, the casualty lists, white flour, and Mrs. Ferguson needing her. Life had never been chaotic like this before. On the farm most days melted comfortably into the next, marred occasionally by a storm or crop loss, but they soon settled back into their placid pattern. A wave of homesickness passed over Margaret, plunging her into a despondency.

Feeling slightly ill from the chicken, she opened the door to the cottage and instantly felt the wrongness in the air. It meant a storm, but whether brewing or over, she didn't know. George sat glumly in the corner with Taylor and Timothy, while Evie pushed a warm cup of milk into Mrs. Brown's hands. Tears streamed down her mother's face. Her father held a letter in his hand, though he didn't look at it. Margaret quietly unwound the scarf from her neck and hung her coat carefully on the hook.

"I'd hoped he would be home for Christmas to visit," Margaret's mother said tearfully. "You think they'd let him see his family before he left."

"I imagine they wanted to get the troops moved before winter sets in," Mr. Brown told her. "It's not worth making yourself sick over, Olivia. He had to go. I don't know how we'll afford it, but we'll try to make a Christmas parcel for him. Bit late sending it, but still he'll know we were thinking of him."

"But I saw the newspaper report of the losses at Dardenelles. He'll be going over there soon," she sobbed.

"Drink up the milk, Mama," Evie said, soothingly.

Mrs. Brown caught sight of Margaret standing by the door. "Edward's gone to England," she cried. She held out her arms and Margaret flung herself into them.

Chapter 12

"And I got a fur muff. A grown-up woman's muff," Pauline emphasized. She picked up a brown fur bundle and stroked it gently. "Also some piano books—"

"Though Mother cancelled our lessons . . ." Mary interrupted.

"Just for a couple weeks." Pauline glared at her sister. "Mother thought with Dad having a holiday, we should have one too. But I will continue practising on my own so I don't fall behind." She popped a peppermint candy into her mouth and sucked noisily. "Now let me see, what else did I get . . ."

Margaret slipped out of her cousins' bedroom. Let Evie sit politely and listen to the list of Christmas gifts. Her sister was always spouting off about being ladylike and mannerly, but if it meant listening to Pauline's boasting, well, she'd rather be rude. She'd go out and play with George and the twins in the snow. As she made her way to the stairs, she realized that even Pauline's bragging couldn't ruin her Christmas day. She still carried a glow inside her.

They'd had their own lovely Christmas morning, made all the nicer by the unexpected gifts she'd been able to give. Mrs. Ferguson had surprised Jean and her with fifty cents each, two days before Christmas.

"Payment for your companion services," she'd muttered, though she'd held on to the coins for a long moment before she dropped them in the girls' hands. "Like she hadn't said a proper goodbye to them," Jean had later told Margaret. "I think she wished she hadn't done it, but she can't take them back now."

Then as they were leaving, Allan had slid another fifty cents into each of their pockets with a cheery "Happy Christmas."

She had immediately run down to the department store where Uncle Harold worked. Just in luck, he'd said. On December 23, the toys in the basement were always put on sale at bargain prices. He had helped her select gifts: two metal trucks, one blue, one red, for Timothy and Taylor; a slide for Evie's hair; a bag of black jawbreakers for George; and two stamps, one for a letter she'd write to Edward as his Christmas gift and another for Catherine. She had wanted to buy a blue wool dress for Mama that she saw in the women's department, but it was too expensive, so she bought a pearl-grey silk scarf instead, though it took half her money. Uncle Harold suggested pipe cleaners for Dad, but Margaret had to tell him that Dad no longer smoked his pipe, tobacco being too dear. Finally she'd settled on a linen handkerchief that she'd secretly embroidered with the initials *M. B.* Uncle Harold had asked for her money and told her she was a good shopper as it came out to exactly one dollar.

It had made Christmas seem *larger*, somehow, to see her presents spread under the tree Dad had got. He'd walked out to the farm where he'd picked apples in October and chopped wood for a day in return for a spruce tree, firewood, and a bag of windfall apples that her mother had made into pie. He could barely hobble the next day, face drawn with pain, but he looked satisfied to see the tree in the middle of the kitchen, its tangy scent filling the cottage. Margaret took a deep breath every time she passed that tree, she loved the smell so much. Evie had tied red bows on it from snippets of leftover wool, and they'd wrapped it in a paper chain they'd made from the Eaton's catalogue and flour glue. A change from using the catalogue's pages in the outhouse, George had told them. Then her presents had gone underneath, to join Mama's and Dad's gifts to each child.

At first Mama had been angry that Margaret had spent her money on gifts. Had even gone so far as to start to say, "That money would have been better spent . . ." when suddenly she stopped, swallowed, and said, "Thank you, Margaret. This scarf will make my old coat quite elegant."

Dad had tucked his handkerchief in his pocket to go to Uncle Harold's for Christmas dinner, making sure the embroidered initials faced outwards for all to see. Uncle Harold had admired it greatly and asked her to do one for him, too.

She clattered down the stairs to the landing and stopped. Uncle Harold's house had a stained glass window of blue and red and yellow overlooking the yard. Placing her face against one pane she peered out to see red snowflakes fall over the vegetable garden. She shifted position and the snow changed to blue. Moved again, and it was yellow. Pretty, she thought, but she liked the proper way snow should be— white. Wouldn't it be nice, though, if life was like that? You could look through the yellow and if you didn't like it, move on to the next colour.

As she squinted out the blue glass again, voices from the living room floated up the stairs.

". . . didn't want to worry you about it at Christmas." Uncle Harold's voice.

"Aren't you too old for the army?" Mrs. Brown asked.

Margaret crept down the stairs and quietly sat on the lowest step, out of view, but able to hear.

"No. No. Just turned forty, Olivia," Uncle Harold protested. "In fact, I hear Prime Minister Borden is thinking of enforcing conscription for all men between eighteen and forty-five to sign up. Whether he'll ever do it, I don't know. I've been thinking about joining up for quite some time now. They said I was a bit stout—" he laughed slightly, "—but army life would soon take care of that. We all have to do our part."

"*Your* part," Aunt Dorothy snapped. "What about your wife and daughters? I've already had to stop their piano lessons in anticipation of your pay cut. We can't survive on what the army will pay you!"

"It's just for a short while, Dot," Uncle Harold assured her. "And I am thinking of you and the girls. You've seen the papers and the posters. Your safety depends on us men getting over there and ending the war. You'll just have to learn to economize. Women all over Canada are doing just that."

Margaret wished she could see Aunt Dorothy's face at those words.

"The store's promised to keep my job open for me for when I come back," Uncle Harold said heartily. "Until then, I guess some woman will do it. We'll have to watch these women, Martin. Working in factories, running the street-cars. They're taking over our jobs."

There was an awkward silence as Uncle Harold realized too late that Mr. Brown didn't have a job to be taken over.

"I have to report in a couple days," he went on quickly. He lowered his voice. "We didn't tell the girls. I told them I'm taking a little holiday. Didn't want to spoil their Christmas. We'll tell them in a couple days."

Uncle Harold was going into the army, and Pauline was sprawled on a bed full of Christmas gifts. How would she take to economizing? Margaret tried to picture her portly uncle in a uniform and found she couldn't. She had thought only young men went into the army and what had Uncle Harold said about conscription? Mr. Riley had told them about conscription, forcing men who wouldn't volunteer to go to war and how shameful a way it was to go to war. She rapidly did some math and with relief decided her father was too old and, besides, with his bad back they'd never take him. She wouldn't want to be Pauline and Mary with their dad at the war. It was bad enough Edward was there. She stood a moment longer listening to George and the twins shouting outside, then went back upstairs and into her cousins' bedroom.

"I—I had to step out a moment," she said.

"I noticed your skirt, Margaret," Pauline said.

Margaret proudly smoothed out the flannel plaid material over her knees. Since she was taller than both Evie and her mother now, she'd outgrown her last dress. Mama had lowered the hem of one of her own skirts, cleverly concealing the turn mark with red braid and given it to her for Christmas. It was the longest skirt she'd ever worn, right to the middle of her calves, and Margaret felt quite grown-up in it.

"Using trim to cover the hem line barely makes it noticeable," Pauline continued. She held a yellow blouse up to her chest. "Mother and Father gave me this waist. Isn't it lovely?"

Instantly hurt, Margaret opened her mouth to tell her cousin she probably wouldn't be getting any more dresses with her father in the army, when a crash from downstairs brought them all to their feet.

"Martin! Harold! Come quick! It's Olivia!" Aunt Dorothy cried.

Margaret and Evie flew down the stairs and crowded into the kitchen. Mrs. Brown sat hunched over in a chair, splinters of china at her feet. Margaret's father knelt down beside her.

"What is it, Olivia?" he asked.

"The baby," she gasped. She moaned and gripped her stomach.

Uncle Harold turned around and saw the gaping mouths. "Right, you children clear out now."

"But, Mama . . ." Margaret began.

Uncle Harold gently pushed them out of the kitchen. "Your mother will be fine," he assured her. He turned back to the kitchen. "I'll get the neighbour's car, Martin. We'll take her to the hospital."

"No, it's too expensive to go to the hospital," Mrs. Brown protested feebly. "I just need to lie down."

"You need a doctor," Margaret's father said.

He helped her walk slowly through the hall. Margaret's heart lurched at the sight of the white, pain-twisted face that barely resembled her mother's.

"The children can stay with Dot," Uncle Harold said, and then they were gone.

"Oh, dear." Aunt Dorothy looked over at the twins and George dripping water on the floor as snow melted from their pant legs. "Oh, dear," she repeated.

Margaret glanced at Evie. She did not want to stay in this house another minute.

Evie squared her shoulders. "I think it would be best if the boys went home to bed," she said. "It's been a long day. Margaret, get our coats please."

"I don't know . . ." Aunt Dorothy began. "Maybe you should stay . . ." she continued weakly. Her eyes went to the door. "Well, if you're sure . . ."

"They sleep better in their own beds," Evie said firmly. "Margaret, George, and I can care for them fine."

Margaret wanted to hug her sister right then, but she ran for their coats instead. She knew she would just burst out screaming if she heard Pauline's odious voice once more.

"Thank you very much for Christmas dinner, Aunt Dorothy," Margaret said politely. That was exactly what Mama would say, she knew.

"You're welcome." The woman fluttered her hands about distractedly. "I'll be by tomorrow to see how you are doing. Or your Uncle Harold will."

They stepped out into the cold air. A full moon glowed white from behind racing clouds, casting dark-blue shadows across the snow-blanketed lawns. Yellow light, warm and friendly, spilled from house windows as they passed, and they huddled closer together. Arriving at the cottage, they pushed opened the door, then stood a moment, reluctant to go into the dark and cold. Finally, Margaret moved inside and lit a lamp.

"George," Evie said, "get the stove going . . . no. Wait." Margaret could see her sister blinking rapidly to hide tears as she glanced at Mama's chair.

"We'll all go to bed instead," Evie decided. "There's no point lighting the stove then. We may as well save wood."

Margaret wrestled the twins into flannel nightgowns and laid them down in their small bed in the corner of her parents' bedroom. Timothy immediately began to cry.

"Maybe we should sleep in here with them," Margaret suggested. "Just until Dad gets home."

Evie nodded.

She ran upstairs, quickly pulled on her nightgown, grabbed her Flower Basket quilt and clattered down the stairs to her parents' bedroom. Scooping up Timothy and Taylor, she jumped into the big bed with them. Evie crawled in the other side and they crowded together to warm the sheets, the quilt pulled up to their chins.

"George," Margaret suddenly called.

Her brother stuck his head around the door.

"Do you want to sleep in the twins' bed?" she asked.

"I'm not a baby," George said disgustedly. "I can sleep upstairs by myself."

"I just thought you'd be warmer down here if we were all in one room," Margaret explained, though part of her felt she'd uttered a lie. She didn't know if she wanted him to sleep in their room for her or for him, but it certainly was not for warmth.

"I suppose," George agreed slowly. "That way I could get the stove going when Dad and Mama come in."

Margaret stared into the darkness, hearing the even breathing of the twins. They were the only ones sleeping, she knew. Was there another Brown being born right now?

"Mama shouldn't have had the baby yet, should she?" Margaret whispered into the bedroom's cold, still air.

She waited with dread to hear what Evie would say. Living on a farm, she was used to births: kittens, pigs, calves. They all knew about births—and deaths.

"I think Mama said the baby would come in late January or early February," Evie said after a moment. "She didn't talk about it much."

Wind rattled the window, blowing past the eaves. Margaret remembered the prairie wind bringing with it the sudden storm and hail which had ruined their crop and forced them to move to Ontario. God had done that, singled out their farm, but He wouldn't let anything happen to Mama and the baby on Christmas night—would He?

The click of the outside door opening brought Margaret instantly awake and sitting up in bed. She looked around, bemused a few minutes, then remembered they were all sleeping in Mama and Dad's bed. Mama! She threw back the quilt and blankets and ran into the kitchen to see her father softly close the outside door.

"Dad!" Margaret cried. "How is Mama?"

"Hush . . ." her father whispered. "Keep your voice down. It's early and I don't want the twins up yet."

He sank wearily into a chair. Margaret shivered, suddenly aware of how cold the room was. She quickly went to the stove, pulled open the iron door at the front, pushed in a few bits of kindling, and lit it. Blowing gently until the flames caught, she then placed a couple sticks of wood on top.

Satisfied it was burning well, she sat across from her father at the table.

"How is Mama?" she repeated.

"She's had the baby—a girl it was . . ."

Was! Dread filled Margaret's heart.

Her father must have seen the alarm in her face, for he immediately shook his head. "No. No. The baby's still hanging on to life. For now. But she was born too early, the hospital says. A little bit of a thing . . ." His voice trailed off.

Margaret nodded. She knew what he meant. She'd seen runts before. The smallest of the litter, they sometimes lived—and they sometimes didn't.

Evie came out of the bedroom, George following, rubbing his eyes sleepily.

"We've got a sister," Margaret told them. "But she's a runt."

Her father frowned at her words, then sighed. He knew the baby was a runt, too. "Mama is very ill. She'll be in hospital for a while."

Taylor and Timothy tumbled into the room and began to clamour for breakfast. Timothy went too close to the stove, his arm touching the hot metal. He began to scream. George grabbed a pail and went outside for water, while Evie comforted Timothy.

"I don't know how we're going to manage . . ." Her father looked around the room as if for inspiration. "I don't even know how I'm going to meet the hospital bills, the medicine, and the doctor . . ." He reached into his pocket and pulled out a small handful of coins. "I have fifty-three cents between ourselves and starvation."

His eyes settled on the chair where Mrs. Brown's unfinished knitting sat. "Margaret, take that wool back to your Uncle Harold's first thing this morning. I don't want to see it in this house ever again."

Chapter 13

"George! Would you hold still? You're going to make me cut it all crooked!" Evie's voice rose with frustration.

George twisted away from her and grabbed the hand mirror, squinting into it. "It looks awful," he cried. "It looks like you chewed my hair!"

"It's not my fault. You won't hold still," Evie argued.

Margaret bent her head closer to her sewing. Thank goodness, she wasn't a boy and could wear her hair long. George was right; Evie had done a terrible job cutting his hair—the front was ragged and the back far too short.

"Mama never had any trouble," George told her.

"Well, I'm not Mama. I'm doing the best I can," Evie said, her voice catching.

Margaret cut a thread and smoothed the row she had finished on the table, pressing the seams to one side with her fingernail. Six rows done now, and one to go, then all that was left was the sashing between the rows and the borders.

Timothy came over to her and pulled at her skirt. "Pick me up, Margaret," he whined. Taylor threw his truck across the room. Margaret sighed deeply. Three weeks Mama had been gone and they were all missing her. Mama was like their glue and now that she was away, they were all becoming unstuck. She studied the newly finished row of geese, her thoughts turning to Saskatchewan. Maybe if they'd stayed there, Mama wouldn't be sick. Maybe by the time she got her quilt finished, Mama would be out of hospital and they could go back home. Like the geese returning every year to their farm, they would, too—once she finished the quilt. George shouted at Evie as Timothy's demands to be picked up grew more frantic. Ignoring everyone, Margaret threaded a needle. She'd better work on it fast. Out of the corner of her eye she saw Taylor's searching hands reach for the scissors. "No. You mustn't touch. They'll hurt you," she scolded.

He began to cry.

"What is all the noise out here?" Mr. Brown stomped into the kitchen from the bedroom.

"Evie cut my hair crooked," George yelled.

"He won't stay still, so of course it's uneven."

"Enough," Margaret's father shouted. "Why are the boys crying?"

"Timothy's ear is aching again and I haven't had time to get the medicine the doctor said he needed," Evie explained.

The medicine. Margaret scrunched down farther in her seat. Maybe Dad wouldn't notice her, because if he did . . . well . . . she knew what was going to happen and she didn't think she could face that again.

"Margaret."

She bent almost in half, hiding her face.

"Margaret," Dad repeated. "You could be more help around here. Put that sewing away and run down to the drugstore and get the medicine for Timothy."

"I'll start supper if Evie goes," Margaret pleaded. "Or George, he could go." He didn't care what people thought. He could just go on pretending everything was fine.

"I said you were to go." Mr. Brown cut off her protests with a slight cuff across her ear.

Tears sprung to Margaret's eyes, but not from physical pain. He'd barely touched her, but the fact he had done it at all—that hurt. Dad never touched them. True, once he'd taken George out behind the barn for a whipping for lying, and the twins got an occasional whack on their backsides if they went too near the stove, but that was all.

She carefully tucked her needle away so the boys wouldn't get at it, then put on her coat and boots. Dread knotted her stomach. She wanted to tell Dad how she'd asked the baker for credit for a loaf of bread yesterday and the man's face had twisted, looking at her like she was something awful he'd found on the bottom of his boots. She'd confided in Jean, who said that happened to her all the time. Her family took credit from stores all over town, moving from one to the next as their credit ran out. She said you soon got used to the looks, but Margaret didn't believe her. You could never get used to people looking at you like that. She wanted to tell Dad, but decided he already knew. She had seen his face when he'd returned from his latest job hunt a week ago. He'd not been out looking for work since.

There was a knock at the door and Margaret pulled it open to see a man in uniform standing outside. After a moment she realized it was Uncle Harold. He stepped into the room, looking sheepish.

"Feel a bit foolish decked out in this thing," he told Margaret's father. "I'm with the 35th Battalion. A private for now, but they told me I'd soon be an officer with my organizational skills and age and all, though I doubt I'll ever see action. Probably work in stores." He seemed almost regretful. "Dorothy will be pleased."

He slapped a newspaper down on the table, pulled out a chair, and sat. "Thought I'd deliver the paper to you in person so you could check the help wanted ads. I don't know if Dot will remember to send it over after I'm gone or not. I'll speak to Mary, or one of the children here could run over and get it at the end of the day."

Margaret immediately decided George would be the one to do that. The less she saw of Aunt Dorothy and Pauline the better.

"Thanks, Harold." Mr. Brown sat opposite him. "Don't worry about it. There's no jobs in the paper anyway. I put my own ad in a couple days ago." He flipped through pages, searching, then stabbed his finger at one. "Here it is. *Middle-aged man wants steady work at inside job.* I have to go down to the newspaper office and check whether they got any responses. It's my last resort. Took all our money so I don't know what we'll do now."

Evie put a cup of tea in front of her father and uncle.

"I'd help you out if I could . . ." Uncle Harold began. "But with my pay cut so much . . . and not knowing when I'll be back . . ."

"No. No. We'll manage somehow. We always do."

"You did a good job on Olivia's cupboard," Uncle Harold said. "Could you do some carpentry work?"

"No one's building houses now that it's winter. I doubt I'd be able to do the work anyway with my back. I could probably make furniture and such except I sold most of my tools." Mr. Martin explained. "I'd given it some thought, though."

"Anything I have, you can use," Uncle Harold offered.

"Thanks, I'll keep it in mind, but you've done enough for us."

Mr. Brown looked around at Evie rocking Timothy and George combing his hair. "Though, Harold, I can't help but think we would have been better off in Saskatchewan. At least we had the garden for food. I found myself actually begging for a job the other day. Begging! Made me feel like I was nothing . . ." His voice trailed off. He suddenly saw Margaret standing at the door. "Didn't I tell you to go to the drugstore?" He half rose from his chair and Margaret scurried out.

She remembered his words as she pushed open the door to Stevens's drugstore and hunched her shoulders protectively around her ears. Dad was right. Every time she asked a store for credit, it felt like she was nothing.

A couple of women stood at the counter talking to the female sales clerk, so Margaret moved to one side, waiting near the plate glass window. The same window, she realized, that Jean's father had thrown a brick through. She thought she could hear the shattering of glass, see silver splinters showering the floor, all for a package of tobacco and a chocolate bar.

Wrapped up in her imaginings, she didn't hear the clerk ask what she wanted. She started when the clerk repeated her question louder.

The two women had not left yet, but stood talking together.

"The doctor said to get this medicine for my brother for his earache," Margaret said. She pushed a note over to the woman.

"You'll have to wait while I get Mr. Stevens," the clerk told her.

Margaret nodded and stepped back, making a show of studying a display of postcards.

"Mrs. George Miller has gone into hospital," one of the women said.

A bell rang as the door opened, and a rush of cold air swept in with a customer.

"Well, you know once you get into hospital, the only way you come out of that place is in an undertaker's hearse," the second woman said dourly.

Margaret's legs turned to ice. Did that mean that Mama wasn't going to get well? That she would come out in a funeral *hearse*?

Blindly, she moved away down an aisle, wanting only to escape the women's voices. A flutter of black at the edge of her vision caught her eye and she could hear the sound of a broom sweeping behind a stack of soap.

"What are you doing here?" A girl's voice spoke at her ear, making her jump. Pauline.

"Getting medicine for Timothy's earache," Margaret muttered.

"Mother sent me to get Catarrhozone for Mary as she isn't feeling well. Influenza, Mother thinks."

Poor Mary, Margaret thought. If there was anything good about being poor, it was that there was no money for medicine to dose them. It seemed everything that supposedly made them better had to make them worse first. All medicine tasted so awful.

Margaret saw Mr. Stevens returning with Timothy's ear drops and hastily made her way to the counter, but to her annoyance Pauline followed.

The drugstore owner set a small bottle down next to the cash register. "Now that will be one dollar," he said.

"Can we put that on credit?" Margaret whispered. She felt heat creep into her cheeks.

"Credit? Isn't your father out of work?"

Margaret nodded, knowing the two women and Pauline were listening to every word.

Mr. Stevens hemmed and hawed for a long time. "I can extend credit until Saturday afternoon," he told her. "But only if you promise to pay me then."

Margaret looked at him dumbly. She couldn't promise any such thing.

"Maybe I could work for you to pay for it," she offered desperately. "Timothy's ear is hurting really bad and he needs the medicine."

"I already have my son to work for me. I don't need other help." He gestured to one side and Margaret turned to see Peter standing with a broom in his hand, watching her. Probably thinking she was nothing, too, Margaret cringed.

"We'd pay you as soon as we could," Margaret told the store owner.

"Some people would rather live on credit and handouts than get themselves a job," one of the women commented.

"You should be down on your knees thanking God that your Irwin has a job, Florence Hadley." Mrs. Ferguson pushed her way between the two women. She dropped coins on the counter. "That'll pay for the ear drops. I'll be thinking about taking my business elsewhere, Mr. Stevens."

Mr. Stevens looked stunned. "But, Mrs. Ferguson, you are one of our favoured customers," he wheedled.

"I said I'd be thinking about it."

She swept out of the store, Margaret scuttling behind her. As the door shut, she heard her cousin say in a loud voice, "We need some medicine for my sister's influenza and we can pay for it."

"Thank you, Mrs. Ferguson," Margaret said.

"I was just doing my Christian duty," the woman told her.

Margaret felt her back go up. She didn't think she wanted to be someone's "Christian duty."

"Besides, Florence Hadley always did get above herself and needs to be taken down a peg or two occasionally, but she is right in some respects—poor people cannot expect others to always pay their way."

Margaret felt her face get hot again. "Dad has never been out of work," she declared indignantly. "He always worked hard on the farm. He hurt his back and can't stand for long or lift anything heavy now." Talking back to her elders, she knew, but she couldn't help it.

She didn't know how to tell Dad about Mrs. Ferguson paying for Timothy's medicine. He wouldn't be happy at all.

"You and that girl can come back and see me Wednesday afternoon," Mrs. Ferguson went on, ignoring Margaret's comments. "You haven't been since Christmas."

"With Mama in hospital, I have to help Evie with the wash. It takes forever," Margaret told her.

They walked in silence until they reached the brick house, then Mrs. Ferguson said, "You and your sister can use my washing machine on Tuesdays. Just Tuesdays, mind you.

That's the only day I can spare it. I'll expect you Wednesday as usual." She climbed the steps to the house. Slowly Margaret made her way across the yard to the cottage and shrugged out of her coat.

"Evie, Mrs. Ferguson says we can do our washing in her machine on Tuesdays," she told her sister.

Everyone stared at her. "That's what she said," Margaret told them, seeing disbelief in their eyes. "She wants me to start coming as her companion on Wednesday afternoons again."

"You don't have to go," her father told her. "I'm tired of everyone bowing and scraping to that woman just because she's our landlady."

"I don't mind," Margaret told him. And, she realized, she didn't. It would be nice to go somewhere quiet and warm for a little while, and work on her quilt. And besides, she thought guiltily, there were sandwiches and tea. "Dad, she paid for Timothy's medicine," she blurted out. "Mr. Stevens wouldn't give credit."

Her father's cheeks bloomed into red. He stood and loomed over Margaret, making her step back. "Why did you let her pay?"

"I couldn't stop her, Dad. She put the money on the counter and left. And Timothy needs the medicine."

"Charity. So that's what it's come to. Charity!" He slammed the palm of his hand down on the table. "I'll pay that old harridan back if it's the last thing I do. I'll get the money somewhere."

He stood and walked over to the cupboard and ran his hands over the wood, considering it. "I'll get the money somewhere. You'll have to stay home from school, Evie, to care for Timothy and Taylor while I look for work. I can't ask Dorothy to watch them anymore."

Evie's face dropped. "I'll never be able to keep up my school work and if I fail, I won't be able to be a teacher."

"It can't be helped. You're the oldest. I can't take any of the others out of school. They're too young and I don't have the money to hire anyone to watch the boys. Margaret will stay home on Tuesdays and help you with the wash." His face turned bleak and hard. "Use Mrs. Ferguson's machine. It'll be easier on you both."

Timothy began to cry and Evie bit her lip as she picked him up, fighting back her own tears.

"Here's his ear drops," Margaret handed the medicine to Evie. Seeing it brought back the conversation and the fear that had filled her in the drugstore—fear that her mother would leave the hospital in a hearse.

"Dad . . ." she began but found that she couldn't ask. She pulled out her quilt top and began to stitch furiously.

"Why you're so darned caught up in that sewing, I'll never know," her father said irritably. "We never see your face, always bent over that thing. There's lots of chores you could be doing to help out instead of working on that."

"I'll help right now, Dad. Really, I will," Margaret said desperately, scared he'd forbid her to work on her quilt anymore and then they'd never get home. At one time she could have told him how she felt, but not now. Not when there was this strangeness between them she didn't understand. She quickly swept scraps into her bag and stuffed it in a corner and put bowls on the table.

"George, get some spoons," she ordered.

George didn't move. "Girls set tables, not boys."

"Get the spoons if you're planning to eat." Margaret glared at him, until he shrugged and sauntered over to the cupboard, returning with a handful of cutlery.

Evie picked up the remaining half loaf of bread and sliced it thinly. "Put another cup of water in the soup," she whispered to Margaret. "Otherwise, it won't go round."

Margaret did as her sister said, stirred a moment to heat it, then ladled the soup into each bowl. Mr. Brown took a slice of bread. "Isn't there anything to put on this?"

"No, Dad, we're out of butter and preserves," Evie said.

He tossed the bread back on the plate, took his spoon, and dipped it into the soup and blew on it, then swallowed. He immediately threw the spoon down. "This is mostly water!" he spluttered.

"I'm trying to make it go around," Evie murmured, close to tears. "There's nothing left to eat."

Mr. Brown pushed his chair back and got to his feet.

"There's Edward's army pay, Dad. He told us to use it if we needed it," Evie ventured.

"I'm not touching his money. I want it waiting for him when he comes back." He grabbed his coat, opened the door, and slammed it shut behind him as he went out.

Margaret shoved her own bowl aside, nodding to George that he could have her soup. She wasn't hungry anymore.

Evie began crying. "I'll never be a teacher. You should be the one staying home." She pointed a finger at Margaret. "You don't like school anyway. You don't want to be anything."

"I do too want to be something," Margaret protested.

"What?"

Margaret couldn't think of a thing she wanted to be.

"That's what I thought." Evie grabbed her school books and went up the stairs.

"I want—I want to work on the farm," Margaret shouted to her sister's back.

"Girls can't be farmers," George told her.

Margaret retrieved her quilting from the corner and picked up two patches and began to sew them together. She had to make her geese fly.

Chapter 14

"Evie, there's a big army parade through downtown, and Uncle Harold's going to be marching in it. We have the day off school." Margaret shook out a sheet, holding an end to her sister to lift over their bed, then let it drop. She rapidly shoved her end under the mattress, watching impatiently as Evie smoothed the creases and carefully folded, then tucked, the sheet in the side.

Straightening, Evie saw the bunched-up cotton by Margaret. "Take that out and redo it," she ordered.

"What does it matter?" Margaret retorted. "You kick all the sheets off when you're sleeping anyway. What's the point of making a bed when you use it every night?" But she pulled the corner out and quickly folded it and tucked it back in. "There! Is that better?"

"Not really," Evie sniffed. "But it will do."

"No wonder you want to be a teacher. You like bossing everybody around."

"I do not," Evie exclaimed.

"Yes, you do," Margaret argued.

"I'm the oldest. It's a big responsibility," Evie said stiffly.

"No, Edward's the oldest."

"Well, Edward's not here!"

Margaret snapped her mouth shut. Evie was right. Edward wasn't here. Her eyes wandered over to his picture propped up on a shelf.

"I miss him, too," Evie said gently.

"Evie, don't you hate it here?"

"Well, the cottage is pretty horrible—" her sister began, but Margaret interrupted. "I mean all of London. School, Pauline, asking the stores for credit."

Evie shrugged as she spread out a blanket. "I have a good friend here and I like my teachers, though I wish I could be at school. Pauline, well, she's taking right after Aunt Dorothy, so she can't help the way she is. I wish I had some of her dresses, though." Evie sighed. "Grab an end of this blanket. No creases."

They lowered the blanket, then smoothed Margaret's quilt over top.

"I guess a place is just what you make it," Evie said suddenly.

Margaret stared at her sister in surprise. "Why, that is just what Grandma Brown would say."

"Is it?" Evie plumped their pillows into place.

"Yes." Margaret ran her fingers over the pieced pink and yellow flowers and brown baskets, marvelling anew at the neat quilting. *Twelve to fourteen stitches to the inch. That's the sign of a good quilter.* But some of the stitches in the quilt were large and uneven, her grandmother's eyes and fingers slowly failing. Margaret didn't mind. They were all the more precious for that. "Do you remember Grandma making this for me, Evie? It was the last quilt she ever made." She herself remembered well. *You're given the bits of material like God gives the bits of life to us, but it is up to you to put them together the way you can best.* A pang went through Margaret. Could even her grandmother have made something out of the bits God was giving them now?

Evie shrugged. "I'm just thankful it keeps us warm. I nearly froze last night. The wind comes right in through the walls! I could have done with a dozen quilts on me."

She was right about that, Margaret silently agreed. The

water in the basin had had a thin crust of white ice on it when they woke up that morning, and even now, while making the bed, their breath puffed white. They were in the middle of a deep late January freeze, as Dad called it. The only warm place in the whole cottage was right next to the stove, and then only your front or back got warm, depending on which faced the stove. But there was one advantage to the cold.

"The rink at Victoria Park is ready for skating. Everybody's going after the parade," Margaret told her sister eagerly. "Say we can go, Evie."

"There's still the stove to be cleaned out and biscuits to be made. Aunt Dorothy gave me some flour, though I sure hated asking," Evie said hesitantly. "And what about the boys? We can't leave them here alone."

"Timothy's feeling better. He and Taylor will like the band and parade. We'll do the chores lickety split. I'll get George to help," Margaret pleaded.

Evie looked doubtful. "I'm not sure what Dad would say. He went out early this morning and he's not back yet."

"You might see your friends from school. They can tell you your homework. Please say yes," Margaret urged her.

Two hours later they stood at the side of Dundas Street, listening to the military band that marched down the middle of the road.

"Why don't the horns stick to their lips?" George asked. "It's cold enough." His nose was bright red.

Margaret puzzled over that question for a moment, then gave up as she saw the men in their uniforms swinging down the street. She stood on tiptoe. "Do you see Uncle Harold?"

George hefted Taylor up in his arms and Margaret picked up Timothy. "There he is," Evie cried.

They called out and waved but Uncle Harold didn't turn his head. "Not allowed to," George told them knowledgeably.

After the parade, they made their way towards Victoria Park. People crowded on wooden benches, putting on their skates. Children darted recklessly through the more demure grown-up skaters, and the people from the parade joined those on the ice until it swirled with colour. George plopped down on the nearest snowbank and struggled to clamp his blades on his boots.

Margaret held out a pair of skates to Evie. "You can go first," she told her sister, anxious that Evie have a good time and stay. There was only one pair of skates, Mama's from when she was a girl, so they had to share. Margaret pulled her younger brothers onto a small patch of clear ice and twirled them around in their boots. With dismay she saw Timothy had lost one of his mittens. They were the only pair he had. She took off one of her own gloves and pulled it over his fingers, shoving her bare hand in her pocket to keep it warm. She looked around the rink and dug in the snowbanks, but didn't find the mitten. She towed the twins back up the path leading into the park.

"Did you lose something?" Peter came up beside her, skates thrown over his shoulder, wool toque pulled low over his forehead.

"My brother lost his mitten." She held up Timothy's hand.

"Hey, I saw one like that near Dundas Street," Peter told her. "I know exactly where it is. I'll be right back."

Margaret waited, shifting from foot to foot to keep them from becoming numb with cold. She hoped it would soon be her turn to skate before she turned to ice herself. She rewound the twins' scarves about their necks and ears, making sure their noses were covered, then pulled her own scarf up over her head.

"Here it is!" Peter ran up with the mitten.

Margaret pulled it over Timothy's hand and tucked the end securely inside his sleeve. She'd have to remember to pin a string on them and thread them through his coat so they didn't get lost again. They headed back to the rink.

"Are you going skating?" Peter asked.

"I'm waiting for Evie to finish her turn," Margaret told him. "We only have the one pair of skates."

"We could go get a hot chocolate to warm us up while we wait," Peter suggested.

Margaret felt her face flush. "I'm not cold. You get some if you want." She didn't want Timothy and Taylor to start yelling for a drink when they didn't have the money.

Pauline twirled up beside them, hands tucked inside her new fur muff. "Come skate with me, Peter."

Peter glanced at Margaret, but she fussed with Taylor's scarf to show him it was of no concern to her whether he skated with her cousin or not. But why did she feel so bad, she wondered, as he made his way to a bench to tie on his skates. Pauline followed, chatting and dimpling at him. She watched him step onto the ice and take a couple practice strides. She turned away, not wanting to see them skating together.

She and the twins wandered around the paths by the edge of the rink. George flew along on their father's skates, the centre of a crowd of noisy boys. He didn't have to wait for his turn to use skates, Margaret thought, thoroughly disgruntled.

She saw Allan sitting on a bench, attention divided between the pad of paper on his lap and the skaters he sketched. She hesitated, not wanting to disturb his work, but he suddenly looked up and saw her, smiled and waved her over. She herded the twins in front of her.

"Aren't you skating?" he asked.

"After Evie's turn," Margaret said shortly. She didn't want to tell him about sharing skates. "I'm watching the boys."

"Oh, yes. I'm sorry to hear your mother is in hospital," Allan said. "Will she be home soon?"

"We don't know."

Allan held out his paper and Margaret saw the skaters weaving an intricate dance on the ice, scarves flying, skirts twirling, heads thrown back. "It's wonderful! They look so real," Margaret exclaimed. "Alive!"

Allan tore off the sheet and smoothed a fresh paper. "Hold still and I'll do you," he said. His hand moved swiftly and Margaret could hear the soft swish of the heel of his palm against the paper as it moved. She felt awkward, not knowing whether to smile or not. She'd never been drawn before. They'd had a family picture done once at the photographers in town in Saskatchewan and Mama had told her to stop grinning. Having your likeness taken or drawn must be a serious business.

"Margaret!"

She turned around to see Jean waving wildly at her from the other side of the park. The girl ran across the rink in her oversized boots, dodging skaters, her long, black coat flapping around her ankles.

"She looks like a crow in flight," Allan commented. He quickly flipped to a fresh page on his pad, his pencil moving swiftly. "Does no one take care of that girl?" he asked under his breath as Jean came up, face streaked with black. "Or give her a bath?"

Margaret didn't answer, knowing he wasn't really speaking to her. "You missed the parade," she told Jean.

"We moved house today," Jean gasped.

"Where are you living?"

"Same street, just down three places. Ma couldn't put off the rent man anymore so we took everything over to our new place this morning. Ma gave our new landlord one week's rent. She always does that. Gives just one week's rent in advance. It fools the landlord into thinking we can pay, then we stay for a few more weeks while she promises him the rent money's coming, until he catches on and wants us out.

Then we move on to a new place and start all over again. Ma says that way she's only out one week's rent for an entire month or so."

Allan stared at Jean a long moment, shook his head, then bent back to his sketch.

"Look at that dumb Pauline skating with Peter," Jean said. "So stuck on herself with that fur thing over her hands."

Margaret inched her nose into the air. "I hadn't noticed."

"He's not holding her hand," Jean told her softly.

Evie skated up to them and sat on the bench next to Allan. "Your turn, Margaret," she said, bending to remove the skate blades from her boots.

"You can pull me around behind you," Jean told her. "I don't have skates but we can do crack the whip."

Margaret took the icy blades, flinching at the cold metal touching her hand, and clamped them to her boots.

"Peter's coming over," Jean warned her. "He's not with Pauline anymore. He's with George."

Margaret didn't answer, continuing to calmly check her boot laces, though her heart hammered against her chest and her fingers fumbled with knots. Numb from cold, she told herself.

"Come on, Margaret. We're going to play tag," George shouted. "Peter is It."

Margaret pulled on her mittens and stepped onto the ice.

"Daddy!" Timothy suddenly crowed. Taylor began to jump up and down on the bench.

Margaret looked around but could only see the rag-and-bone man's horse and cart on the road passing the park, though today the horse only wore a hat, no stockings.

"Daddy!" Timothy shouted again.

"Oh!" Evie breathed in a short gasp.

Puzzled, Margaret followed her sister's gaze to the driver's seat of the cart. There perched on top was her father!

"That's your dad? Your dad's the rag-and-bone man?" a voice shrieked. Children crowded around them.

"Of course not," Margaret said desperately.

George's mouth dropped open.

A snowball sailed through the air and hit the side of the cart.

"You boys stop that!" Margaret's father yelled, pulling on the reins and stopping the horse.

Margaret felt her entire body go numb, but not from cold this time. She flopped down on the ice and savagely pulled off the skates with trembling fingers.

"Are you the new Johnny?" someone shouted.

"What happened to the old one? They finally take him to the lunatic asylum?"

Margaret stalked across the rink, not noticing when a skater rammed hard into her, nearly knocking her off her feet. She had to get away.

"Wait," Allan called. He held out his pad of paper. "Don't you want your picture?"

She began to run.

"Margaret," Mr. Brown shouted.

She ran past the cart, refusing to look at him. How could he do this to them? Her father, the rag-and-bone man. Only a crazy person was the rag-and-bone man. She'd never live this down. Never.

Chapter 15

"I'll take this letter up to the hospital to show to your mother." Margaret's father slid the white envelope into his pocket. "Not that it will bring much comfort to her."

A letter from Edward had arrived, containing the news that he was at a camp in southern England for further training before heading to the frontline. *From our camp we can see the coast of France on a clear day. Imagine, we are only a few hours away from the firing. Where I am is some of the prettiest scenery in England, making it hard to imagine a war is on. I went to Dover the other day with some of the fellows and saw a number of torpedo boat destroyers. A ship fresh from France was unloading some of the wounded. The boys were shot up pretty bad. I can't wait to get over to the front and see the war for myself. Last night a German Zeppa dropped bombs on the camp, and a couple of our boys were killed. We covered all the windows with blankets for tonight in case we get visited again. I hope they lose their way.*

The week before had seen the arrival of another letter, from Catherine, telling her friend that she'd been by the Brown farm and that dirt had drifted high against the side of the house and tumbleweeds had overrun the yard. It'd made Margaret feel sad, but at least she knew the buildings and house still stood. There would be somewhere to go back to come spring.

"Say hello to Mama, and the baby," Evie said to her father.

Mr. Brown waited a moment. "Do you have a message for your mother, Margaret?"

Margaret shook her head, keeping her eyes on the piecing in her hand.

There was a long silence. "There's no shame in an honest day's work that is putting food in *your* mouth!" he said, voice tight with anger.

Tears sprang to Margaret's eyes, blurring the patches in front of her until they swam blue and brown, but still she didn't speak. The door slammed behind her father.

"How can you do that to Dad?" Evie scolded. "It's just for a few weeks until Johnny's up and about on his feet again from his pneumonia, and it's money coming in. You should be ashamed of yourself."

That was the trouble—she was drowning in shame: shame that she had only one skirt to wear to school day after day, shame that they lived in a house with an outdoor pump, shame that Dad was the rag-and-bone man, and, worst of all, shame that she hurt her father so much. If only Grandma Brown was here to talk to. She'd know how to put the shame to rest.

"Come on. We better get going if we're to use Mrs. Ferguson's washer," Evie said.

Thank goodness, they had to do the washing and she didn't have to go to school today. As soon as she set foot on the playground yesterday, she'd felt the difference. The girls ignored her most of the time, but yesterday they'd giggled and whispered behind their hands. She'd glanced over to the boys' side to see George standing alone, bewildered and lost.

"Her father's crazy," a voice had said as she'd passed through the yard. She cringed now, remembering her shame.

Jean had come over to join Margaret, but she'd swept right by the girl saying, "I might be the daughter of the rag-and-bone man, but at least I'm not a criminal's daughter."

Thinking about that now, remembering Jean's devastated face, she felt the shame come back in waves. She hadn't meant it. Just had lashed out, feeling so hurt.

She piled clothes into a large basket and heaved it onto one hip and went to follow Evie out of the door. "Straighten your hair. It's sticking up everywhere," Evie ordered. She dipped her hand in the water pail and flattened Margaret's hair.

Margaret pulled back. "I can do my hair myself," she protested.

"Well, then do it! And your petticoat is showing beneath your skirt."

Margaret hitched it up as best she could with the basket in her arms.

"Do you know where George is?" Evie asked.

"I saw him outside in the yard. I'll go look." He'd be glad he wasn't going to school today, either. She rounded the side of the cottage to see George sitting with his back against the shed, head hanging down.

"Your pants will get all wet sitting in the snow like that," Margaret exclaimed.

"I don't care," George mumbled.

"Well, you'll care if you catch cold and Evie starts dosing you," she threatened. "We're going to do the washing, and you need to watch Timothy and Taylor."

George climbed slowly to his feet. As he did, Margaret caught sight of an ugly purple bruise swelling on his cheek.

"What happened?" she cried.

"Nothing. Just a fight."

"What were you fighting about?"

"If you need to know, Miss Nosy . . ." George grabbed the hat from his head and pointed to his hair. "About this! Everyone knows Evie cut it. And Pauline's been going around telling everyone Dad's the rag-and-bone man. The boys say Dad's a lunatic like Johnny."

"Even Peter?" Margaret asked, holding her breath and wondering why she cared so much about George's answer.

"Peter didn't say anything. Didn't tease me, but didn't stick up for me, either. I went over to the school and settled things up at recess. Mr. Riley saw me fighting. He'll probably tell Dad," he added glumly. "Why are they acting like this?"

Margaret had never seen him so upset. She remembered him saying he ignored what went on around him and pretended things were fine. Obviously he couldn't do that anymore and it was hitting him hard.

"I don't know why they're acting so dumb. We're no different this week than last. I'm sorry, George." Margaret couldn't think of anything else to say. "Maybe we'll go back to Saskatchewan in the spring. You and I are getting bigger. We should be able to help out a lot on the farm. Despite what you say, girls can work on a farm. I don't need to go to school after next year."

George looked hopeful for a moment, then the corners of his mouth turned down. "We'll never go back. We're stuck here forever. I wish I was like Edward and could go to war." He wandered towards the cottage.

Margaret stared after him. So Peter hadn't helped George. A stab of disappointment took her by surprise with its intensity. She followed Evie to the brick house and waited while her sister knocked at the door. Hilda opened it and waved them into the kitchen. She pointed towards the washer set in the middle of the room, then left.

"Doesn't she speak?" Evie asked.

"I've never heard her say anything. Maybe her tongue was cut out as punishment for lying."

"Don't be so silly," Evie scolded. "You're not a child anymore. You should act your age. Start sorting these clothes while I fill the tub with water."

Margaret grimaced at her sister's back as she took George's

pants and added them to a pile of her father's work shirts. Evie was born old!

The sorting done, she watched as Evie dumped carefully hoarded soap shavings into the washing machine, followed by water from the warming tank on the back of Mrs. Ferguson's stove, and stirred it a moment with a long stick, before adding the boys' pants. She turned the handle on the side of the tub, churning the clothes together.

"This is a lovely machine. It moves so easily," Evie admired the shining tub. "And the clothes wringer is right on top instead of separate. That makes less work."

Hilda came back and put a kettle on the stove.

"It's a beautiful kitchen," Evie told the woman shyly. "It must be a pleasure to cook in and you keep it so nice."

Hilda smiled briefly. She leaned over the washer, took the stick, and prodded the wet clothes a moment, nodded her approval, and stepped back. The kettle whistled shrilly and the woman quickly measured tea into a pot and filled it with water. She set it back on the stove to steep while she sliced bread, buttered it, and placed it on a tray with a small pot of jam and a china teacup. She filled cups with tea and placed them on the table, setting a slice of bread beside each, then motioned to the girls to sit down before placing the teapot on the tray and leaving.

"Is that for us?" Evie said.

"I guess so."

They sat down at the table, Evie glancing around the orderly kitchen. "It's nice here," she said, sighing. "Imagine someone fixing your tea and serving it to you. I'd love a maid."

Margaret decided not to tell her sister about her teas with Mrs. Ferguson.

Hilda returned a few moments later, put on her hat and coat, and let herself out the door.

"Thank you," Evie called to the woman's back.

"It might look nice, but it's a strange household," Margaret told her.

"We better get the washing finished." Evie stood up from the table. "You clean these cups up—and do a good job that even Mama would like."

"Evie," Margaret said as she dried the cups. "Do you think Mama is getting better?"

"Dad says she is. It's just taking a while to get her strength back. He says the baby's getting stronger, too."

"Have you been to see her?"

"Mama? No. Dad said they wouldn't let us children see her in case we brought in germs."

Margaret carefully put the cups away. Dad wouldn't say Mama was getting better if she wasn't, would he?

"Evie," she said suddenly. "It's been almost four weeks since the baby was born and she doesn't have a name yet."

"Maybe Mama and Dad didn't name her in case she didn't live," Evie said, her voice matter-of-fact. She pushed clothes through the wringer. "Keep turning that handle, Margaret, so all the water gets out!" she exclaimed. "It's harder to lose a baby once it's named. That first load is ready for the line now."

"The machine sure is a lot faster than using that old scrub board," Margaret said. "If for nothing else I'll thank Mrs. Ferguson for that."

"Margaret!" Evie looked scandalized. She cast a quick glance at the closed door leading into the rest of the house. "Can you not hold your tongue? What if she hears you? And whatever you do, don't put Dad's combinations on the line. We'll hang them and our corsets and drawers inside by the fire. Mama would die of embarrassment if we hung our underwear outside."

Margaret hauled the basket of wet clothes outside and began to peg them to the line. She hoped Mama would be home soon and she hoped the baby would live. Hope. She stood still, one of the twin's rompers dripping in her hand. Hope! Everybody should have a name. She'd call the baby Hope. Just to herself, of course.

Carrying the empty basket back to the brick house for another load, she saw the curtains part and a black shadow in the window of the parlour. Margaret waved, but the figure moved back and the curtain fell back into place. Margaret shrugged. She'd be seeing Mrs. Ferguson soon enough anyway. She had to go over there tomorrow afternoon.

"Margaret," Evie shrieked from the back door, arms waving frantically. "You've put my brassiere and corset on the line!"

Margaret carefully laid the triangle templates on the scraps in an effort to get every bit of material from them. She was fast running out of remnants, but if she was frugal, she thought, eyeing the pile, she'd have just enough for the borders to go around the quilt. They would be flying geese, too. Four rows of patches were sewn together now, but three long pieces of uncut fabric were needed to run between each row for sashing. She had no idea where she'd find them and so had decided to piece the borders in the meantime.

Jean was reading to Mrs. Ferguson and her, though she seemed distracted, stumbling often over words. She'd been like that at school today, too, Margaret realized, and Miss Simmonds had become quite impatient with her. Guiltily, she remembered brushing past the girl in the playground. Jean had avoided her most of the day, adding to Margaret's guilt. Maybe Jean was too upset to read.

"You may as well stop," Mrs. Ferguson said peevishly, when Jean repeated a sentence twice to get it right. "I don't know what's the matter with your tongue today."

"I'm tired is all," Jean said.

"Well, have a good sleep before you come here. It's the

least you could do, seeing as how the only thing I ask you to do is read." The woman got up and crossed to the table where Margaret had her rows spread out. She picked one up and squinted at it. "Your stitches are very neat and even. You're a good seamstress."

Jean came over and dropped the book on the table, scattering pieces to the floor. "Sorry," she said, bending to pick them up. "You could set yourself up as a dressmaker," she told Margaret. "You could be your own boss and make a living for yourself."

Margaret shot a quick glance at the girl. Maybe Jean wasn't mad at her, after all. Relief flooded through her. What had Jean said? Make a living for herself. She felt a small flutter of excitement in her stomach. She'd not thought about making her own living. Evie had always known she wanted to be a teacher, but Margaret had always thought she'd just be married like Mama, live on a farm and have children. But she wouldn't mind sewing clothes for people and the money might come in handy, married or not. But what would her husband say about her working? Dad hadn't been too happy about Mama doing knitting. Most men didn't like their wives working. It seemed to take something away from them.

"Whatever happened to girls wanting to stay home and take care of a family?" Mrs. Ferguson said, her thoughts obviously following the same path as Margaret's. "In my day, girls didn't think about flying aeroplanes, being nurses, or being the boss of anybody."

"In your day they didn't have aeroplanes," Jean retorted. "Why shouldn't girls become pilots or be bosses? We're just as good as men at doing things, sometimes better. More and more men are going away to war right now, and women are taking over their jobs in factories and on farms. They're driving ambulances and doing some of those jobs better than the men!"

Margaret heard the door open quietly and someone come in. She glanced up to see Allan standing by the bookcase, listening to his mother and Jean.

"God wants women to stay at home, doing what their husbands ask of them. No matter what Mrs. McClung and her like say."

"I doubt God wants that," Jean replied. "Maybe men want that. Besides, everything's changing these days with men going off to war and being killed. And I'm not sure God wants that, either."

"Well said, Jean." Allan laughed and came into the room. "You have a debater here, Mother. She keeps you on your toes." He flopped down onto a sofa.

"Well, I think she should learn to hold her tongue!" Mrs. Ferguson said heatedly. "God is on our side in this war, the right side. He will help our men to cleanse the world of evil. You can't be a good Christian if you are only partly loyal to God and your country."

"Perhaps the Germans think God is on their side, too," Jean told her. "And what if they're right?"

Margaret paused in her sewing. She'd never thought of the Germans as people before, going to church, shopping, school. They were a faceless enemy. Was there another girl, overseas, piecing a quilt and praying her brother would be safe as he fought against the Canadians? Every Sunday in church the minister said God was fighting right alongside their men, but what if God wasn't involved in the war at all and the men fought alone—on both sides? She felt a deep emptiness. Could Jean be right? Her eyes lingered on her friend's face as the girl continued arguing with Mrs. Ferguson. She appeared tired, white, and peaked, except for a red mark across one cheek.

"What happened to your face?" Allan asked suddenly, seeing it also. He heaved himself from the sofa and pulled Jean to a window.

"I walked into a—a door," Jean said hurriedly, turning away.

"A door with fingers," Allan commented, studying the redness. He exchanged a glance with his mother. She pursed her lips, but merely said, "Go ask Hilda for the tea, Jean."

"We must do something," Allan said as soon as the girl had left the room.

"There's nothing we can do. It's not our place to interfere," Mrs. Ferguson told him. She fell silent, tapping a finger on the arm of her chair. "How's that girl do in school?"

"She gets good marks in English and history. Miss Simmonds gives her extra books to read," Margaret replied. "Lately, though, she's been too tired to do her homework and Miss Simmonds has been mad."

"Mother, someone is hitting that girl. We have to do something," Allan insisted.

Margaret looked up, shocked. Of course. How could she have not known? Jean wasn't accident prone, she moved too quickly and surely for that. But who was hitting her?

"It's between her and her family," Mrs. Ferguson repeated. "Maybe she needs discipline. Heaven knows she's wild enough."

The agitated tapping continued until Jean returned with Hilda and a trolley piled high with the tea pot, cups, sandwiches, and small cakes. Jean quickly downed two cups of tea and crammed a handful of ham sandwiches into her mouth.

"Your manners are atrocious," Mrs. Ferguson scolded.

"Sorry, Missus. I was hungry," Jean mumbled through a full mouth.

"And do not speak with food in your mouth."

"Sorry," Jean repeated, then snapped her mouth shut as she realized she'd spoken with it full again. Her foot banged impatiently against a chair leg and she began to scratch her head.

"Stop that infernal noise and stop fidgeting," Mrs. Ferguson ordered. "And when was the last time you washed your hair?"

Jean shrugged, moving restlessly.

What, Margaret wondered, was bothering Jean? She couldn't sit still.

Mrs. Ferguson replaced her cup in the saucer with a rattle, picked up a napkin, and patted her mouth. She rang a tiny bell beside her and Hilda came in. "Clear these things away." She turned to the girls. "You can both leave now. I don't hold with ill-mannered people."

"Mother," Allan protested, then shook his head helplessly.

Margaret quickly put her scraps back into the bag, folded the strips on top, and pulled on her coat. Jean was halfway out the room by the time she finished. As they passed through the kitchen to the back door, Hilda suddenly appeared and thrust two packages wrapped in brown paper into their arms, ushered them outside, and closed the door behind them.

Margaret pulled a corner of the paper away. "It's leftover sandwiches," she told Jean. "I guess she made too many. Evie will be able to put some in Dad's lunch for tomorrow."

Jean carelessly pushed her sandwiches into one of the deep pockets in her coat. "Never mind that now," she said. "I have something important to tell you and . . ." She stopped a moment. "And something special to ask of you." She glanced up at the brick house and plucked Margaret's sleeve. "Come away from here. I don't want anyone eavesdropping."

She pulled Margaret behind a tree out of view of the house and cottage. Margaret huddled close to the trunk. It helped somewhat to break the wind, but she could still feel cold swirling up beneath her coat hem. She hoped Jean would hurry up and tell her what she wanted to say, but Jean suddenly became tongue-tied. Finally, she took a breath. "My dad's out of jail," she said all in a rush. Her eyes stared at a spot above Margaret's right shoulder. "Ma says we're not to see him. She says he doesn't deserve to see us, shaming us by going to jail. But I . . . I want to see him. I miss him."

There was a lot of pride in Jean, Margaret realized. She had trouble asking anyone for help.

Margaret nodded for Jean to go on, still uncertain what she wanted her to do.

"My brother Richard says Dad's staying under the bridge by the river for a couple nights, hoping Ma will change her mind about him. But he's only staying two nights. Says he's jumping a train and going to Halifax to join the navy. I have to see him, Margaret. If I don't see him now, I'm afraid I'll never see him again. I wonder . . ." She stopped, bit her lip, and looked directly at Margaret. "Will you come with me Friday night to the bridge?"

Chapter 16

A whirlwind of snow blew into Margaret's face as she slid down the icy slope into black beneath the railway bridge. She couldn't believe she was actually there with Jean, out so late at night. Mama would have a fit if she knew, but hopefully she would never find out. Or Dad, for that matter. If he discovered she'd crept out of the house after all the family was asleep, well, it didn't bear imagining what he'd do.

The world, she discovered, took on a different guise after sunset. Towering pines, friendly by day, became darkly ominous by night. Far off a dog barked, its howl immediately picked up and echoed by a second dog, then a third. The scent of wood smoke mingled with the damp smell of the nearby half-frozen river.

Her feet suddenly slipped from beneath her and she slid on her back the rest of the way down the incline. Picking herself up, Margaret wiped snow from the back of her coat, then looked around for Jean. Her mouth dropped open at the number of men sheltering beneath the bridge. Most were huddled around two huge fires, but here and there on the ground a dark shape slept alone, bundled up against the cold. Never had she imagined that this other sad world existed so close to her own.

Jean edged her way to the first fire to search for her father, and Margaret hurried to catch up, not wanting to be left alone in this increasingly frightening place. Unease gave way to panic as she squeezed past the men. Faces, at first glance all seeming old, were, in fact, young, prematurely aged by cold and weariness and hunger. What had brought them to this place? She wanted to run home to huddle beneath Grandma Brown's quilt, but knew Jean needed her.

"Dad!" Jean suddenly cried and threw herself into a man's arms.

Margaret stood back, watching them, then wormed her way closer to the fire as her fingers began to go numb from cold.

"What are you doing here, girl?" Mr. Thurlowe asked.

His voice carried a slight musical lilt. Irish or Scottish, Margaret decided. She'd have to ask Jean some time.

"Richard said you were here. He said you were going away and I had to see you before you went," Jean replied.

"I don't imagine your ma knows you're out this late," Jean's father scolded.

Jean hung her head. "She said we weren't to see you."

"Well, then, you shouldn't be going against your ma's wishes."

"I know, Dad, but . . ."

Mr. Thurlowe suddenly swept Jean up in a hug that left Margaret's eyes stinging with an unexpected fierce longing. When had Dad last hugged her? Putting Jean back down, Mr. Thurlowe turned his daughter's face towards the fire. "What's this on your cheek? This bruise? Has your ma hit you?"

"Don't mind, Dad," Jean said dismissively. "The baby was fussy one day and Ma was beside herself. She didn't know what she was doing."

Margaret felt shock jolt through her, yet she wondered why. She knew someone was hitting Jean, but she never thought it had been the girl's mother! Mama would cuff them occasionally, and then only for a good reason, but never hit so hard as to leave a bruise.

"She shouldn't be taking it out on you," Mr. Thurlowe said angrily. "I should be there to keep things from happening. I'm so sorry, girl. I've let you down."

And he wasn't the only one, Margaret thought. She still had not apologized to Jean.

"As I said, don't mind, Dad. I'm fine. I need to talk to you." Jean looked around at the listening men, then pulled her father to one side. Margaret stumbled along behind on icy feet.

"Oh, Dad," Jean said. "This is my friend, Margaret Brown. She came with me tonight to keep me company."

Mr. Thurlowe stuck out his bare hand and Margaret pushed a mitten into his.

"You are lucky, Jean, to have such a friend as would come with you here. I don't expect your family knows you're out, either." He frowned at Margaret, then his lips twitched upwards. "But I'm glad to meet you."

Margaret stared at her feet. "She's not that lucky, Mr. Thurlowe. I was mean to Jean the other day and I'm sorry." Her teeth chattered with cold as she forced the words through frozen lips.

Jean stared at her. "Oh, that on the playground? I'd forgotten all about it. You were mad at the world, and I just happened to be in your way that day."

Margaret looked back at her friend in surprise. How could Jean forgive so easily? A mother who hit her, a father just out of jail, no decent clothes, yet she didn't hold a grudge against anyone, and certainly not against life. Margaret mulled this over, all the while shooting furtive glances at Mr. Thurlowe. This was the closest she'd ever been to a criminal. He was not what she had expected—a criminal should be someone large, with perhaps a bushy beard and a mean glint in his eyes, not this slight, exhausted-looking man with the soft, singing voice.

"Dad," Jean said. "You can't go away."

"Your ma won't have me back. She's made that plain. I'm going out east to join the navy. They'll take just about anyone with the war on, and I'm hoping that far away they won't ask too many questions about me. I'll get regular pay then and I'll send it back to your ma. Maybe that will make her think kinder of me—and you," he added.

"Then take me with you," Jean demanded. "I can get work in a factory, or go overseas with the Voluntary Aid Detachments. The women volunteer to help the nurses, or drive ambulances."

Her father shook his head. "No, girl. You're too young."

"I could lie about my age and if you back me up, they'd believe me."

"No. You have to stay here. Go to school. Keep out of your mother's way as much as you can." His voice became grim.

"But, Dad . . ."

"I can't take you, Jean. I don't know where I'll be. You've a good head on you, girl. Of everyone in the family, you are the one who could make something out of yourself. Don't lose that opportunity."

Tears streamed down Jean's face. "I'm going to be a nurse, Dad."

"Good. You hold on to that, then. I'll be back," he promised. "Once I get into the navy and send some money back to your ma and the war is over, maybe things will be different."

"You'll write and tell me where you are?" Jean held on to his hand.

"As soon as I get settled I'll send a letter . . . but in the meantime . . ." He clapped his hands together to warm them. "It's very late so I'll walk you two ladies home. You first, Margaret, if you'd show me the way."

As they passed through the deserted city streets, Mr. Thurlowe asked Margaret questions about her family, and she found herself telling him all about Mama in the hospital and the new baby she'd named Hope and Dad out of a job. He'd nodded his head knowingly at that. Turning down the street leading to the brick house, Margaret stopped abruptly and gave a tiny shriek as a figure loomed out of the darkness in front of them.

"Dad," Margaret breathed. Her heart began pounding.

"Where have you been?" her father yelled.

"I . . . I went with Jean to see her father under the bridge by the river," Margaret stammered.

"It was my fault, Mr. Brown," Jean cried.

"I'm Frank Thurlowe." Jean's father stepped forward and held out a hand.

Margaret's father hesitated a moment, then briefly shook it.

"I expect you know all about me. Most people do." Mr. Thurlowe held his head higher. "I got out of jail a couple days ago, and I've been living rough, trying to straighten a few things out before I go away. I don't approve of what these girls did tonight," he went on. "Jean knows better, and she shouldn't have dragged your daughter into it, but I will tell you that Margaret here is a very loyal friend."

Mr. Brown said nothing, his eyes roaming up and down the man.

"I feel easier knowing Jean has a friend like her, as I'm leaving tomorrow. Heading to Halifax by boxcar and joining the navy."

"I'm sorry, Dad," Margaret whispered. She stepped to her father's side. She felt his body rigid with anger.

Jean and her father turned to leave.

"Mr. Thurlowe," Margaret's father said suddenly. He pulled thick gloves from his hands. "Take these. It's a miserable night, and if you're travelling tomorrow, you'll have more need of them than I do."

Mr. Thurlowe hesitated.

"My oldest son, Edward, is in England waiting to go overseas. Perhaps you will run across him some time and do him a kindness."

Mr. Thurlowe nodded and accepted the gloves, then he and Jean disappeared down the street.

Mr. Brown turned to Margaret. "Into the house! Now!" Margaret scurried indoors to find Evie sitting near the stove, face twisted with worry. She'd obviously woken and, not finding Margaret beside her, had sounded the alarm. "Go to bed," Mr. Brown told her. Evie scrambled up the stairs.

Margaret slowly unwound her scarf, waiting for the storm. She heard a chair being dragged out from the table and anxiously turned to see her father sitting, staring at her.

"Do you know how dangerous it is for a young girl to be out walking the streets at night?" he asked sternly. "Especially down at the river where those homeless men are? Can you imagine what your mother would say?"

"I'm sorry, Dad. It's just Jean asked and . . ."

"And you thought it was more important to do what Jean asks than what you know is right."

"Well," Margaret began then stopped. She hadn't really thought at all, she'd just gone. "Her ma wouldn't let her see her dad before he went away, so she asked me to go with her," she explained. "She just wanted to see him. That felt right, too, Dad."

"Maybe her mother had a good reason for not letting Jean see him."

"She said he'd shamed the family, that's why. Because he'd been in jail. He didn't look like a criminal, did he?"

"He looked like a poor and unhappy man," Dad said, his tone softening. He splayed his fingers out on the table and stared at them. "We all look poor and unhappy." He sat a long moment. "So you're Jean's friend. I don't expect that girl has many friends."

"No," Margaret agreed.

"And you? Do you have many friends?"

"Well, Jean, and Miss Simmonds, my teacher, is nice to me, and Mrs. Ferguson and Allan," she added.

"Mrs. Ferguson?" Her father sounded surprised.

"I guess." Margaret shrugged. "She's sort of a friend. She talks to me anyway. Dad, Jean's mother hits her."

"Hits her?"

"She's got a big bruise across the cheek. She's had others."

Mr. Brown looked slowly around the room, shaking his head. "What a mess I've landed us in."

She watched her father's face become closed and knew he'd shut himself off from her once again.

"Dad," she said hesitantly. "Can I still be friends with Jean?"

He looked at her blankly, then nodded his head. "I guess so, seeing as she's the only friend you have, and you're her only friend. Now get to bed and never let this happen again," her father ordered.

Margaret began to climb the stairs, when her father's voice stopped her. "Just a minute."

He pulled a bundle wrapped in brown paper from his coat pocket. "This is for you."

Margaret came back down the stairs and untied the string holding the package together. Cloth spilled out, enough to make the sashing between her geese rows.

"A lady was throwing it out and I thought it might be of use to you."

She stood fingering the cloth. It was good quality, silky smooth to touch. "Thank you, Dad. I'm sorry I was rude about you being the rag-and-bone man. It's just the others at school made fun of me and George and . . ."

"I know. I know. But I'm doing what I have to do to keep food on the table. Now it's late. Get along to bed."

In the bedroom, Margaret's cold fingers fumbled with the buttons of her nightgown. She felt chilled right into her bones and couldn't stop shivering, but didn't think it was all from the frigid air. She slipped into bed beside Evie.

Evie gave a cry. "Your toes are like ice."

"Sorry," Margaret mumbled, pulling her feet away.

"Was Dad really mad?" Evie asked.

Margaret thought a moment. "I don't know." In fact, she wished he had been mad and yelled at her. Mad she understood, but not this troubling confusion she felt now.

"You can lay your feet next to mine," Evie offered after a moment. "They'll warm up faster that way."

Slowly Margaret's shivering lessened and she began to feel drowsy. Fragmented images crossed her mind: men crouched before a fire beneath the bridge; Mr. Thurlowe; Edward with a bayonette; Dad bewildered and sad; Jean's battered cheek; and Grandma Brown leaning over her patchwork. *Quilting is about working with bits and pieces. You gather them up and stitch them into an orderly pattern.* But what if the pieces were too many, too small, and too scattered to ever put together?

Chapter 17

"Terrible situation, this." Margaret's father tapped a finger on an article in the newspaper. "Imagine that quartermaster at the barracks stealing meat meant for the soldiers and selling it for profit! Have you heard much about it at the camp, Harold?"

"There's been some talk, but the army likes to keep it fairly quiet," Uncle Harold replied. "Don't want to lower morale. But I do know there are more charges pending. My feeling is there's more to it than a couple soldiers looking to make an easy dollar. Here we are trying to win a war, and our own people taking advantage of the situation. Takes all kinds."

Margaret moved closer to the stove for warmth, holding her sewing at an angle to catch the fire's dim light. War, she was fast discovering, was more complicated than school or church made it out to be. The lines between right and wrong, so clear to her before, were fast becoming blurred.

It was dark as night in the cottage, even though it was just after lunch. The day's light had been swallowed by wind-driven snow rattling against the window. She could sit at the table where Evie was studying under a coal oil lamp, but an icy draft came in under the door frame, so Margaret huddled near the stove. A sudden shriek of wind reminded her of prairie blizzards—howling storms sweeping from the north unchecked across the flat land, hurling snow into a blinding white wall. As she joined pieced geese blocks to form a border, they rose living from her quilt and took flight against a clear Saskatchewan sky, their cries echoing over the farm and spring green fields. She could see them so clearly her lips parted with joy, then suddenly clamped together again as fancy fled and reality took hold once again. She wasn't in Saskatchewan. She sat in a small, cold, damp cottage in Ontario, listening to Dad and Uncle Harold talk about the doings at the army camp.

Margaret had been surprised to see her uncle at their door during such a storm but he said he felt a bout of restlessness and needed to get out. Aunt Dorothy and Pauline would give anybody cabin fever, Margaret thought uncharitably.

"What's that you're working on, Margaret?" Uncle Harold asked suddenly.

"Her Flying Geese quilt, Uncle Harold," Evie answered, raising her head from her school books. "She works on that thing day and night."

Margaret spread out the rows she'd sewn together so Uncle Harold could see.

"That's lovely," he exclaimed. "Bit hard on the eyes, though, working in that dim light. Too bad that old woman couldn't extend the hydro out here."

"Just as well," Mr. Brown told him. "I couldn't afford it right now."

"Still no sign of a job, then."

Margaret's father shook his head. "I keep hearing about all these jobs going begging now that all the men are gone, but I can't find them. Still, I imagine something will turn up, if we can survive until then. At least the little bit from the cart helps, but Johnny will be back soon since he's finally on the mend."

"Well, if the man would wear a coat in winter . . ." Uncle Harold's voice trailed off. "I'd like to help you out, Martin, I really would. But with my pay cut so much, Dorothy is beside herself trying to make ends meet already. I had no idea it would be so difficult. Perhaps I shouldn't have signed up . . ."

"We'll be fine, Harold. Though I do appreciate the offer. Besides, if conscription comes in, you'd be going anyway and volunteering is a better way to become a soldier."

"Dad," Evie said suddenly. "There's a job for an upstairs maid at the Tecumseh Hotel—"

"No," Mr. Brown interrupted. "I don't want you working at a hotel cleaning up after who knows who."

"It'd just be Saturday afternoons until you get a job," Evie went on. "Margaret could watch the boys."

"No," their father repeated. "You start working and we'd come to expect the money and then you're trapped. You'd never go back to school and become a teacher like you want. As I said, we'll manage."

An uncomfortable silence was broken by another piercing shriek of wind.

"Listen to that storm!" Uncle Harold exclaimed. "Too bad your quilt wasn't finished, Margaret. I'd wrap it right around me, it's so cold out there."

Finishing the quilt. Now that was a problem Margaret had been trying to avoid. The material Dad had got had been enough for sashing and a bit left over for the borders, but she still needed a lot of material for the backing.

"Where are you going to get the material to finish your quilt?" Evie asked, voicing Margaret's dilemma.

"I don't know. I was hoping I could find an old sheet, but there's no spares these days," Margaret replied. "I thought I'd use the blanket from our bed for the middle as it's pretty threadbare. But the backing's a problem. I don't know where I'll get it. I need a lot of material and I've used up pretty much everything in Grandma's bag, so I can't even piece one together." She'd lain awake nights trying to figure this problem out.

"Red's mine!" A loud cry from the corner of the room

brought all their heads around. Timothy tugged on a toy truck in Taylor's hand. Margaret set aside her border. "I'll see to them, Evie. You keep on with your studying."

She caught Evie's look of gratitude and felt a pang of guilt. She knew deep down it wasn't all concern for Evie that caused her to jump up to quiet the twins. It was mostly a desire to get back on Dad's good side. She didn't want to do anything that would remind him of her escapade last night, not that he was likely to forget.

She plunked the boys in chairs at the table and gave them a cup of warm milk to drink. Once they finished it, they'd probably sleep and she could work some more on her quilt.

Uncle Harold shifted in his chair, cleared his throat, paused, then asked. "Any more tea?"

That hadn't been what he was going to say, Margaret thought, but she jumped up, pulling the teapot from the stove. She carefully refilled her father's and uncle's cups.

"You've got a good helper here, Martin," Uncle Harold said.

"Yes," Mr. Brown agreed dryly, giving Margaret a knowing glance.

Not fooled one bit, Margaret knew. She looked into the empty teapot and hoped Uncle Harold wouldn't ask for another cup. That had been the last of the tea, but they'd offered it to Uncle Harold like Evie said Mama would want, even if it meant none left for themselves tomorrow.

"I was up seeing Olivia yesterday," Uncle Harold went on. "She's looking better. Any idea when she'll be let out?"

Margaret felt a rush of anger. If Uncle Harold could go visit Mama in hospital, why couldn't she? Maybe just children carried germs, not grown-ups. Still, it felt good to hear Uncle Harold say she seemed better. She missed Mama so much.

"I don't know. They can't get that fever of hers to stay down two days running. She's had a rough time of it."

"And the baby?"

"Hanging on. A fighter for such a tiny mite," Dad said, pride and wonder softening his voice.

Hope! Margaret thought. She has a name. Hope! But she couldn't tell Dad she'd named the baby. Her shoulders drooped as if beneath a great weight. She wanted to see Mama. Wanted to see baby Hope with her own two eyes. Only then would she believe they were getting better.

Uncle Harold scraped his feet across the floor and cleared his throat again. "I came over for more than a visit, Martin. I came to say goodbye. I've got my orders to be mobilized. That's why I was up seeing Olivia. I have two days' leave, then I'm going Tuesday morning."

They all stared at him. They'd known he'd go sometime, but now that it was here, it didn't seem real.

"How's Dorothy taking it?" Dad asked.

"Not saying much, but she sure isn't happy. I'm telling the girls tonight. I wonder . . ." he stopped, then started again. "With your situation and all . . . I really hate to ask this of you, but I wonder if you'd keep an eye on them for me? Make sure things are fine with the house, if they need help."

"Certainly," Margaret's father readily agreed. "We'll do everything we can."

"I really do appreciate it. Don't like to think of them on their own."

Margaret glanced at the clock sitting on Mama's cupboard, startled to see the hands had marched so far ahead; nearly two o'clock! It had seemed like night all day long, making it difficult to keep track of the time.

"I have to go to Mrs. Ferguson's," she announced. She looked over at Evie, suddenly troubled. Evie was trying desperately to keep up with her school work from home. "Unless you need me, Evie."

"Go," Dad said. "I'll keep an eye on these two." He pulled

Taylor onto one knee, then Timothy to the other. Taylor struggled to get down. "They look just about due for a nap anyway. Though why you keep seeing that old battle-axe, I'll never know. By the way, I haven't seen George all day. Do you know where he is?" Mr. Brown asked.

"He said he had some things to see to," Margaret told him.

"Probably gone sledding with the boys," Uncle Harold said heartily. "They're the only ones fool enough to be out in this weather. Must be great to be young, eh, Martin?"

Margaret smiled, but privately doubted it. She'd seen George's face when he left. He wasn't out playing with friends. He'd gone to settle some differences again. He stood by himself in the schoolyard these days, ignoring the others. She'd noticed Peter go over a couple times, but George wouldn't even look at him, so the boy no longer tried. She wished she could do something to make it easier for him, but she wasn't allowed on the boys' side. At least she had Jean, though the girl's attendance at school was patchy these days.

She put on her coat and boots. "Goodbye, Uncle Harold."

"Goodbye, Margaret. I'll write and let you folks know how I'm doing, but you have to promise you'll write back."

"We will," Margaret assured him. Her eyes lingered a moment longer on him. "Maybe you'll meet Edward," she croaked, barely able to force the words past the huge lump in her throat.

"Maybe I will," Uncle Harold said. "You be a good girl now."

Margaret nodded and left the cottage before she burst into tears and made him feel bad. She plowed through knee-deep snow, clutching her bag with her quilt and scraps tightly so the wind wouldn't snatch it from her. She felt a guilty relief to be leaving the cottage, knowing she'd have an uninterrupted hour to sew at Mrs. Ferguson's. She'd make it up to Evie, she told herself, by doing supper so her sister would have more time to study. Her mind ran over their remaining food stores, wondering what she could make from a few turnips, potatoes, and a bit of flour. Potato pancakes, she decided as she knocked on the back door of the house. They'd be filling.

Hilda opened the door immediately and held it against the wind, gesturing to Margaret to hurry inside. Margaret said a polite hello, then took off her outer clothes, being careful not to drip melting snow on Hilda's clean floor before making her way to Mrs. Ferguson's parlour.

"Where's that other girl?" Mrs. Ferguson demanded.

"I expect the storm is keeping her home," Margaret said. She hoped it was the storm anyway. Had Jean's mother found out about her being out late last night?

Hilda brought in the tea things right away, instead of waiting until the end of their visit as she usually did.

"She wants to get home before the snow gets worse," Mrs. Ferguson explained. "We'll have it in a bit. I guess you'll want to work on that quilt rather than read to me," she grumbled.

"I'll read if you like," Margaret said.

Mrs. Ferguson waved an arm. "Never mind. I know you really want to work on that sewing you cart with you everywhere." She leaned wearily back in her chair by the fire, eyes focused on the picture of Blair.

Margaret felt uncomfortable and compelled to speak. "Where's Allan?"

The woman grimaced, got to her feet, and moved stiffly to the fireplace, poking randomly at the fire. "Around somewhere. Drawing pictures, no doubt. That's all he seems to do. Weather's hard on my legs," she complained. She picked up the photograph from the mantel and studied it. "He was popular at school, Blair was. Handsome. All the girls thought so." She shoved the picture towards Margaret.

He did have good looks, Margaret agreed, except his chin seemed a bit weak.

"High-spirited, too. He could get into more trouble, but then he'd just smile and make you forget all about it. Couldn't smile his way out of death, though." Mrs. Ferguson abruptly placed the picture back on the mantel, then crossed to a table and opened a drawer. She took out a piece of paper, unfolded it, and handed it to Margaret. "That's all I have left of him. The chaplain who buried him drew me this map to show me his grave in France near Ypres. He'll never come home and I'll never go there to see him."

Margaret took the paper, noting how soft the creases were from being folded and unfolded many times. She studied the rough pencil drawing and with a finger traced a curving line, a road, she guessed, to an X marking the grave site. A small box next to it indicated a church.

"At least he's in a regular graveyard," Mrs. Ferguson said. "I heard many of our dead just sank into the mud where they were killed and disappeared. Doesn't seem right they're not in a church burial yard, but I suppose God knows where they are."

Margaret handed back the map. Mrs. Ferguson squinted at it, then refolded it and placed it in the drawer.

"Allan couldn't hold a candle to Blair," she said finally. "To think he's the one left."

Margaret's mouth fell open.

"Don't go gaping like a fish," Mrs. Ferguson said impatiently. "I'm not telling the Lord who He should or should not take. I'm sure He has his reasons."

"For which I am glad, Mother."

Margaret jumped and turned in her chair to see Allan standing inside the door. She hadn't even heard it open.

"Don't look so upset, Margaret," Allan assured Margaret. "I told you Blair was her favorite."

He sat down and Margaret poured him a cup of tea,

noting that despite his calmness, his face was white. His hand trembled slightly and tea spilled into the saucer. Margaret felt a surge of anger at Mrs. Ferguson. She was horrible. Mama had six children, no, seven counting Baby Hope, but she certainly didn't have any favourites! Even Grandma Brown didn't have favourites in her quilts. *I love them all equally, Grandgirl. Each is different, but that's what makes each special in its own way. Like asking me to pick one grandchild over the other. It can't be done.* She glanced at Allan's face again. It must hurt terribly to know your mother preferred your brother to you.

"What are you going to do with that quilt you're making?" Allan asked, seeing her distress and trying to distract her.

"I'm not sure," Margaret answered hesitantly. She didn't really want to discuss the quilt with them. "Give it to Dad perhaps. He likes geese. We used to watch them fly every spring and fall over our farm in Saskatchewan. We'll see them again when we go back."

"Go back? I thought you had an auction," Mrs. Ferguson said.

"We did," Margaret said. "For the household furniture, the equipment, and a few animals."

"Well, I expect your farm was auctioned then, too. That's what usually happens in these cases. Probably the bank auctioned it off right after you left."

Margaret sat stunned, holding her teacup halfway to her mouth. It had never occurred to her that the farm wouldn't be theirs for them to go back to when Mama got out of hospital. She had thought it would always be there for them. She put her cup down into the saucer with a rattle and pushed the sandwich away. She didn't have any appetite left.

"That cupboard your father made," Mrs. Ferguson continued. "Do you think he'd sell it?"

"What?" Margaret said. She couldn't seem to think clearly.

"Take the cotton out of your ears, girl. I asked if your

father would consider selling that cupboard he made. The workmanship in it is excellent. I'd like that cupboard. I'm sure your father could probably do with the money, what with your mother in hospital running up bills and him out of work."

"I don't know," Margaret said. "Mama loves that cupboard. I don't think he would sell it." She desperately blocked the image of her father standing in front of the cupboard. *I'll get the money somewhere.*

"Well, you tell him I'll give him a good price, more than what's fair for it if he wants to consider it. You can't hold on to things just for sentimental value when you can barely pay the rent."

Margaret stared at the woman and got to her feet. "I'll take the tray out and tidy up," she said stiffly.

Tears threatened to spill over as she washed up the cups and wiped down the counters. Allan came in and took a cloth and began to dry.

"You don't have to do that," Margaret told him.

"I know."

They worked together in silence, then Allan spoke softly. "I know you won't believe me, but Mother was not always this way. Not until Blair died. I mean, I always knew Blair was her favourite, but she never came right out and said it before. Strange as it may seem, she does love me, Margaret. I had hoped having Jean and you here might help her get over his death a bit and it seemed to be. She was taking more of an interest in things."

Margaret didn't know what to say. She only knew Mrs. Ferguson now, not before, and she'd already made up her mind that she was never coming again. The woman was horrid.

"I'll be leaving soon . . ." Allan continued.

"Are you going back to Montreal?"

Allan dried the cup, not answering right away. "I hate to

think of mother on her own when I'm not here. Promise me you'll keep visiting her?" he asked.

Margaret remained silent.

"Please?"

She bit her lip, then sighed, giving in. "I'll keep coming only because you asked. I can't speak for Jean."

She hung up the dishcloth, then gathered her quilt bag.

"You love that quilt, don't you?" Allan said.

"It's going to get us back to Saskatchewan," Margaret told him.

"Mother was too blunt, but she is probably right. I imagine your farm was auctioned off by the bank when you left. You should ask your father. He'd know. I don't want to hurt you, but I don't want you building up false hopes," Allan told her.

Margaret put her boots and coat on, then picked up a small parcel of sandwiches Hilda had left for her on the table and put it on top of the bag.

"No," Margaret told him calmly. "As soon as I finish the quilt, we're going home."

Chapter 18

Margaret watched silver drops of water meander down fogged classroom windows, leaving jagged streaks in their wake. The end of January had brought a sudden thaw, melting snowbanks into brown puddles, both in and out of the school. The school furnace blasted heat, unaware of the unseasonal warmth, making the rooms stuffy and hot. She shifted slightly in her seat so she could see Jean. The girl had been away all week, only returning to school that Friday morning. She was worried about Jean, as, she realized, was Miss Simmonds, who threw several quick glances at the girl. This was the first Margaret had seen her since their late-night adventure under the bridge and she was anxious to have a talk. She shifted again, making the wooden desk creak loudly. Miss Simmonds frowned. Finally, the dismissal bell rang and everyone leaped from their seats.

Stepping over discarded boots and abandoned mitts, Margaret shrugged her arms into her coat and waited for Jean as the cloakroom emptied. She peered in through the tiny window in the classroom door to see Jean returning a book to Miss Simmonds. The teacher held out another one, but the girl shook her head, then made her way out of the classroom.

"I waited for you," Margaret told her as Jean pushed open the door.

"Thanks," Jean mumbled, unsmiling.

She looked different today, her face set.

"Have you been sick?" Margaret asked. "I'm glad you're back."

"Sort of sick," Jean replied, not offering anything more.

Bewildered, Margaret led the way out of the corridor's gloom into the playground. Blinking against the afternoon light, she covertly studied Jean's face, relieved to see no fresh bruises.

"Feels like spring, though I know it's not really. It's like a promise you know isn't going to be kept," Jean said. She took a deep breath and pushed a stray strand of hair behind her ear and Margaret's heart sank to see a yellow swelling on the girl's temple.

"Was your Dad really mad? I didn't mean to get you in trouble," Jean apologized.

Margaret shrugged. "He was mad at first, but not now. What about your mother? Did she find out?"

"Yes. She found out," Jean said shortly.

Shouting on the playground momentarily distracted Margaret.

"I'm sorry. What did you say?" Margaret asked.

"I said I'm leaving," Jean repeated. "I'm going to hop on a freight train tonight, and I'm going to find my dad in Halifax. Once I'm with him and he sees I can take care of myself, he'll let me be a V.A.D. helping the nurses. I understand they give the V.A.D.'s food and a bed."

Margaret's eyes widened. "You can't run away. You're not old enough."

Jean pulled her hair up on top of her head. "This way I look nearly sixteen," she said.

Margaret looked at her doubtfully. With her dirty hair and the yellow swelling and the tired purple circles under her eyes, she barely looked older than Timothy and Taylor! "Aren't you scared?" she asked.

"You have to have courage if you're going to be a nurse, so I can't be scared," Jean told her.

"I'd be afraid anyway," Margaret replied.

"You're not to tell anyone," Jean said. "Promise."

After a moment, Margaret reluctantly agreed. "Promise."

Suddenly, her cousin Mary appeared in front of them and tugged on Margaret's arm. "Come quick. George is in a fight. You have to stop it before the principal comes out and gives him the strap."

"Jean . . ." Margaret threw an agonizing glance back at the girl as Mary towed her away. "Don't go until tomorrow night," she called over her shoulder. "Come to Mrs. Ferguson's tomorrow afternoon." She cast about desperately for something, anything, to make her friend stay. "Hilda will probably have some sandwiches for you. You'll need food for the train." She let Mary pull her away.

George was definitely in a fight, Margaret saw, and he didn't seem to be winning. Peter Stevens sat on top of him, holding George's hands down at his sides, but at least he wasn't pummelling him. George squirmed and shouted, face red with the effort to free himself. Pauline stood near the line separating the boys' and girls' sides, cheering Peter and talking loudly to her friends.

"They are family, I'm ashamed to admit. It's a cross we bear. Mother says poor people are shiftless and always trouble," Pauline announced.

Long-stifled hurt and anger rose in Margaret. She shook Mary's arm off and she waded into the circle of boys surrounding the fight, pushing them aside to reach George. She grabbed Peter around the chest and pulled him off, falling backwards into a heap with him on top of her. She heard a loud ripping sound and hoped it was her petticoat and not her skirt giving way.

"What a disgraceful display! Her drawers are showing!"

Pauline put her hands over her face. "Her mother was hoping she'd learn some manners from me, but obviously she hasn't. I'm embarrassed she's my cousin!"

Margaret struggled to get up, but found herself pinned beneath Peter's leg. She shoved hard to get him off.

"Enough!" A man's voice shouted.

The schoolyard fell silent. Peter's weight shifted and Margaret scrambled to her feet to find the principal, Mr. Riley, glaring at her. Miss Simmonds was behind him.

"Not only are you fighting, Miss Brown," Mr. Riley bellowed at her, "but you are also on the boys' side of the playground. You have shown a flagrant disregard for the rules, young lady."

Margaret stared at her feet, face flushed with shame. She hadn't even thought about being on the boys' side; she had only been concentrating on getting Peter off George.

"You, you and you," Mr. Riley pointed at Margaret, George, and Peter. "Into my office now."

Margaret followed George's back, too humiliated to look at her classmates.

"Poor as paupers," Pauline whispered, as they passed.

Margaret whirled around. "And you will be soon, too," she hissed. "With your dad gone to the war, you're going to be poor as paupers, too, until he gets back—*if* he gets back."

Pauline's face went white with shock.

Immediately, Margaret wished she could take the words back. She'd said the first thing she could think of to hurt Pauline. She opened her mouth to apologize, but Mr. Riley stood at the door, face furious. "The rest of you go home," he ordered.

"She'll get the strap," she heard someone say. "Imagine, a girl getting the strap."

She filed into the school behind George and Peter. She had thought things couldn't get worse, but they had.

"If I could speak with you a moment, Mr. Riley," Miss Simmonds said.

The principal nodded. "Sit," he ordered and Margaret lowered herself onto the bench, George and Peter sitting on either side. She noticed the lace of her flannel petticoat hanging down and one of her stockings laddered.

The wood edge of the bench cut deep into her thighs as she stared at the black lettering on the closed door in front of her. PRINCIPAL. She'd never been in trouble at school. Voices murmured through the office door. What was going to happen to them now? She'd only been in the principal's office once before when she had delivered a note to him from Miss Simmonds. She'd seen the narrow strip of black leather hanging in full view beside Mr. Riley's desk. It was okay if you were a boy to get the strap—almost a badge of honour—but a girl! A girl getting the strap was disgraceful. She'd never be able to show her face at school again. She jutted her chin out. Well, she'd just stay home and take care of the twins and Evie could go to school, or—or she could run away with Jean. Her heart sank thinking of her friend leaving and a tear trickled down her cheek.

"I didn't mean to get you in trouble," Peter whispered beside her. "Don't cry."

"Why were you fighting George?" Margaret asked.

"I wasn't. Not really. He just came at me all at once."

She turned to George, sitting on her other side. "Why were you fighting Peter?"

"Pauline said Peter would never look at you twice because you were poor and plain looking and big as a house," George told her. "I couldn't get at her because she was on the girls' side and, besides, Dad says you shouldn't hit a girl, so I got Peter instead."

"I never said that," Peter protested loudly.

"Shh . . ." The school secretary frowned at them over the top of her glasses.

Margaret felt her face getting hotter and hotter. She shifted slightly away from Peter. If only the floor would open and swallow her. Poor and plain and big as a house, all because of Grandma Brown's people. But they'd also given her quick hands to make tidy stitches, except right now she'd give up her quilting to be small and pretty!

"I really didn't say that," Peter whispered out of the side of his mouth, leaning over her to speak to George. "Margaret might be plain, but she's certainly more fun than that fussy Pauline. I never saw your cousin holding on the back of a streetcar sliding or sneaking into the theatre like your sister did. And I don't care a whit if you're poor."

They were talking through her like she wasn't sitting there, Margaret thought, shame turning to anger.

"I didn't know that. I'll tell Mr. Riley it was all my fault," George said softly. "That way only I'll get the strap."

"Naw. We'll share the blame. Then we can show off our red hands to the others." Peter and George grinned at each other, irritating Margaret further. They might be able to show off their red hands, but she'd never live down hers. And Peter thought her plain, though, she allowed, better than Pauline.

Miss Simmonds opened the principal's door and gestured for them to come in. Margaret's heart thumped against her chest as they lined up in front of the principal's desk.

"One of the rules of this school, as every student knows, is no fighting. I won't have students acting like hooligans. You have broken the rules and will take the consequences," Mr. Riley said sternly. He stood and took the strap from its hook. "Hold out your right hands, palms upward."

Margaret slowly extended her arm. Never had she thought she'd be standing in the principal's office getting the strap.

Miss Simmonds cleared her throat noisily.

Mr. Riley looked at Margaret. "Put your hand down, Miss Brown. I'll deal with you later."

Margaret's arm fell like a dead weight. She stared at the knots in the principal's wood floor, wincing at the sound of leather hitting flesh, three times for each boy, but felt better when she saw Peter wink at George as they left the office. Suddenly she found herself alone with her teacher and the principal.

"Miss Simmonds says you are a good student, Miss Brown," Mr. Riley said. "Respectful and helpful, though you are having some difficulty adjusting to our school. She thinks this incident is only a one-time occurrence and will not happen again. I also understand your mother has been in hospital some time now."

Margaret nodded.

"Times get hard, but we can't let that affect our good behaviour."

Margaret nodded again.

"I'm not going to give you the strap, but I am going to send a letter home to your father, telling him what happened here today. He can punish you as he sees fit." He handed her a folded sheet of paper. "I don't want to ever see you in here again."

"No, sir," Margaret said.

Miss Simmonds put her arm around Margaret's shoulders and led her from the principal's office. "I'd like to send a note to your father, also," she said. "Please wait here a moment, Margaret."

She soon returned, holding out a small envelope. "Please give this to him. I explained what happened and that the fault was not entirely yours. I probably shouldn't have, but, well, just give it to him."

"I will," Margaret assured her, taking it. Two letters. She didn't know what Dad would say. Never before had she brought letters home from school.

"It will get better, Margaret," Miss Simmonds told her. "We all just have to hang on for a while and have a little faith."

Faith!

"Miss Simmonds . . ." Margaret stopped.

"Yes?"

"I just thought you should know that Jean's mother hits her," she finished in a rush.

"I know," Miss Simmonds said quietly. "Unfortunately, there's nothing I can do, Margaret. I give Jean books and help her keep up with her studies. Jean is very bright and I'm hoping in the end she can find the good life she deserves. I am glad, though, that Jean has you for a friend."

Margaret debated telling Miss Simmonds Jean was leaving, but she had promised the girl she'd tell no one. She walked into the deserted playground and found herself immediately pounced on by George and Peter.

"So what happened?" George demanded, then stuck out his hand. "It didn't barely hurt," he bragged, but immediately plunged his hand into snow.

"Did you get the strap?" Peter asked.

"No, but I have two notes to take home to Dad," Margaret told them.

She looked George up and down. "I don't know whether to be mad at you or not," she said.

"Oh." Peter slapped a hand against his forehead. "George, I almost forgot to tell you. Dad said the newspaper is looking for delivery boys, if you want a job."

"Want a job? I'll go see them right now." George whooped and ran off, arms pumping wildly, sore hand forgotten.

"I'm glad you didn't get the strap," Peter said, then suddenly grinned. "Who'd think you could fight like that— and on the boys' side, too." He fell into step beside Margaret.

"I really didn't say those things to Pauline," he told her.

"I know," Margaret said, glumly. But he still thought her plain.

"Are you going to the church sleighing picnic Sunday afternoon? I have the fastest coaster in London and you can ride on it if you like. Jean too," he offered. "Some of the girls are afraid of sledding, but it shouldn't scare you two."

"What about Pauline?" Margaret asked. "Won't she be going with you? You went to the movies together."

"No, we didn't," Peter said disgustedly. "We arrived at the theatre at the same time so she said we should sit together. I couldn't think of a polite way to say no. She's always doing that."

"Well, then I'd like to go sledding," Margaret told him. "But I doubt Dad will let me go after he sees these letters. Peter," she went on, "why are you nice to Jean? Most of the other kids aren't, and she broke your dad's store window and stole from him."

Peter shrugged. "Jean's dad did that, not Jean. Besides, you always know where you stand with her. I don't have to be dodging her all the time or be polite like I do with some of the other girls."

Margaret studied Peter as he bent and picked up some snow, forming it into a ball. He was very nice. Maybe he'd get taller some day and she wouldn't seem so big.

"Did you know Pauline invited me to a party for Valentine's day? A sweetheart party! Have you ever heard of anything so silly? But, Jean," Peter continued, "Jean is just herself. You can take her or leave her, she doesn't really care, and I like that. You're sort of the same way too."

He made it sound like a compliment, and Margaret found herself smiling and feeling lighter.

"I turn off here," Peter said.

"I'll let you know about the sleighing picnic," Margaret promised. She suddenly remembered the letters in her hand. Chances were slim she'd see Peter on Sunday.

She let herself into the cottage to see Mrs. Ferguson standing in the kitchen talking to her father. She scuttled into the room; she'd never told Dad about Mrs. Ferguson's offer to buy the cupboard.

"I'll give you a good price for it," the woman said. "I imagine the money would come in handy."

"Yes, it would," Mr. Brown admitted. "But I'll have to think about it awhile. I'll let you know ."

Mrs. Ferguson opened her mouth as if to pursue the matter, then suddenly nodded and pushed past Margaret without a glance at the girl.

"Dad! You can't sell Mama's cupboard!" Margaret protested as the door shut behind the woman.

"I might not have any choice if we want to pay next month's rent."

Margaret took a deep breath, remembering the notes. "I have a letter from the principal," she said miserably.

Her father flipped open Mr. Riley's letter and quickly read it, his face clouding over. "A daughter of mine fighting like she was brought up in the street," he thundered. "Is that how your dress got ripped?"

Margaret plucked at the waistline of her skirt. She had forgotten it had been torn. "And Miss Simmonds said to give you this," she said, holding out the second letter. Her father grabbed it from her hand, but didn't bother to open it.

"More trouble!" he yelled.

"No Dad," Margaret interrupted. "Miss Simmonds said she explained in her letter about the fight. If you'd just read . . ."

He wasn't listening. "What's the matter with you? Sneaking out at all hours of the night, fighting at school. Go up to your room! Now! Get out of my sight!"

Margaret flew up the narrow staircase. She flung herself down on the bed, then sat up and wrapped her grandmother's quilt around her. Usually feeling Grandma Brown near quieted her mind, but not today. *After my baby died, I couldn't do anything but quilt. Not the tidying, not the baking or the other chores, but I could quilt. I nearly quilted my fingers to the bones. I quilted that horrible pain into an ache.* Suddenly she threw the quilt off. She'd work on her sewing. The sooner it was done, the sooner they could leave this awful place. She pulled out the bag from the corner beside her bed, then knelt down beside it, puzzled to see her scissors lying on the floor nearby. She always put them away carefully, mindful of the twins getting hurt.

She unfurled a long border strip, then froze. Tiny pieces of material fell to the floor. Frantically she pawed through the bag and found one long border of geese cut. Timothy and Taylor must have got upstairs when Evie wasn't looking, found her scissors, and cut her quilt top! She let the coloured scraps trickle through her fingers. They were too small to be pieced together, and she didn't have any more material to make a new border. Her shoulders heaved in huge sobs. She'd never finish the quilt now. They'd never get home.

Chapter 19

Margaret's feet dragged across the yard to the brick house, leaving black trails through a new-fallen layer of snow. January thaw over, they'd once again plunged into winter, the sky above swollen with grey clouds. She didn't feel like seeing anyone, let alone Mrs. Ferguson, but she'd promised Allan, and, besides, it might give her one more chance to talk Jean out of leaving. She didn't know what she'd do there, since she didn't have her quilt to work on anymore. After seeing the border all cut to pieces, she'd bundled up the top and thrown it into the farthest corner under the bed, then flung herself down and cried until she fell asleep. Evie must have taken off her stockings and tucked her in, because when next she woke, it was morning. Dad had already left to drive the rag-and-bone cart. She wished she had seen him as she still didn't know what punishment he was giving to her for fighting.

"Margaret!" Jean beckoned from behind a clump of shrubbery at the side of the house.

Margaret hurried over to her, relieved to see her friend hadn't left yet. Maybe she'd changed her mind. "Are you coming to Mrs. Ferguson's?" she asked.

"In a minute," Jean said. "I have to hide this."

Margaret looked at the small bundle Jean was thrusting into the centre of the bushes and felt her heart sink. Obviously, Jean was still set on going.

"Remember. You promised not to tell anyone," Jean reminded Margaret. "Especially *her*." She nodded towards the house.

"Please don't go, Jean," Margaret pleaded. "Maybe your father will come back and things will get better."

"Things never get better, only worse," Jean said bitterly. Margaret had no answer for that. Jean was right.

"I'll only stay at Mrs. Ferguson's a bit," Jean continued. "Long enough to get some sandwiches for the train."

They left the bush, arriving at the back door in time for Hilda to pull it open. The woman scrutinized Jean's and Margaret's faces carefully. Like she knew, Margaret thought guiltily, feeling her cheeks become hot. She hated secrets. Jean seemed unconcerned as she pushed past the woman, kicked off her boots, and led the way to Mrs. Ferguson's parlour.

"I was beginning to think you two weren't coming," Mrs. Ferguson complained. "Well-brought-up girls are not tardy."

"We're not well brought up," Jean replied flippantly. "Do you want me to read?" She went over to the bookcase, stood a moment looking longingly at the books, then took down *Jane Eyre*. "We might be able to finish this today," she said.

"Where's your sewing, girl?" Mrs. Ferguson asked Margaret. "Is that quilt done? You'll have to start something else. Idle hands are the devil's work."

"I—I," Margaret began, feeling tears prick. "Timothy and Taylor got into my quilt and cut part of the border. I can't repair it and there's no more material left to make more. Every spare scrap we have goes into patches for our clothes these days."

"Oh, well. No doubt you'll collect more as time goes by," Mrs. Ferguson said. She motioned to Jean to start reading.

"You don't understand," Margaret interrupted. "I have to get my quilt finished. It's a Flying Geese quilt. Geese migrate in the spring back to Saskatchewan. If I get that quilt finished, Mama would get out of hospital and we could go back to Saskatchewan, too."

"You place that much faith in a heap of material?" Mrs. Ferguson snorted.

"Yes," Margaret said shortly.

"That's almost as foolish as this girl wanting to fly in an aeroplane."

The door suddenly swung open and Hilda wheeled in a trolley piled with sandwiches, small cakes, a teapot, and cups. Behind her, Margaret could see the figure of a man. A man in uniform. Allan!

"Isn't this a bit early?" Mrs. Ferguson pointed out to Hilda.

Hilda ignored her, placing the platter of sandwiches on the table.

Mrs. Ferguson glanced over at Margaret. "I don't know what you're looking at, but keep that mouth open and you'll catch flies in it . . ." Her voice trailed off as Allan came into the room. One hand flew to her chest as she half rose from her chair.

"Allan! What are you doing?"

"I've joined up, Mother. Last week. Doing my bit, you know." He stood awkwardly a moment, then sat in the nearest chair.

Jean, Margaret saw, had taken the opportunity of confusion to slip a couple sandwiches into the folds of her skirt.

"I thought while I was there I'd do some sketching, record the glories of the war for all eternity," he told them, voice deceptively cheerful. He gestured towards the teapot. "Margaret, could you pour me a cup please, and one for Mother?"

Margaret leaped to her feet and filled two cups.

"What about your studies?" Mrs. Ferguson asked.

"They'll be waiting for me when I get back," Allan replied.

"Or I might even stay on in Paris after the war and study there."

Mrs. Ferguson's eyes turned to the picture of Blair.

"I intend to come home, Mother," Allan said gently. "And until then, Margaret and Jean will keep you company. I've already extracted a promise from Margaret and . . ." He set down his cup, looking around the room. "Where is Jean?"

Margaret started from her chair. She'd been so caught up with Allan, she hadn't noticed Jean slip out of the room. "She's running away," Margaret blurted out.

"Running away?" Allan repeated.

Hilda stopped gathering the tea things and stood still.

"She's tired of her mother hitting her. Her father is out of jail and he left last week for Halifax to join the navy. Jean's going to take a train, too, and try to find him and then get work as a V.A.D."

"As a V.A.D.? Foolish girl! She's far too young," Mrs. Ferguson exclaimed. "They'll turn her away."

"Then she'll be left on her own in a strange city," Margaret cried. "Isn't there anything you can do to stop her?"

Mrs. Ferguson got up and walked over to the window, pulling the curtain aside. "Those brothers of yours are trampling up the yard," she complained. "They should know better than to walk on frozen grass!"

"Mrs. Ferguson!"

The woman turned from the window. "There's nothing I can do. I can't stop her mother hitting her. People don't interfere in other people's business. Especially poor people's business."

"I'm poor, too," Margaret shouted. "But that doesn't mean we're no good and don't count. It just means we fell on hard times." She jumped to her feet. "Jean's smart. She wants to be a nurse and I want to finish my quilt so my family can go home. *We* have hope so we're not all that poor. You are the poorest of us all. Sitting around moaning over your lost son, when you have Allan right here. You made him sign up! You! Now he's going away. You're poorer than any of us because you'll be left all alone." She dashed tears from her eyes. "I'm going and I'm never coming back! You can even tell my dad about me sneaking into the theatre. It doesn't matter anymore. I'm sorry, Allan, but I have to break my promise." She pushed open the door to leave.

"That girl is speaking the truth."

Margaret stopped. Hilda! She did talk.

"Oh, do be quiet," Mrs. Ferguson snapped.

"I've a right to my opinion," Hilda told her.

Margaret didn't wait to hear any more, but rushed through the kitchen, grabbing her coat and boots.

She ignored the carefully wrapped parcel of sandwiches sitting on the table and rushed back to the cottage. She began to turn the doorknob to go in, then stopped. There was something she had to do. *Don't put off until tomorrow what can be done today. It doesn't make it easier.* She may as well get it over with because as Jean said, nothing ever got better, it only got worse, and this was the worse things had ever been.

She slowly walked down the street, thinking frantically about what to say, but still had thought of nothing when her feet stopped outside Uncle Harold's house. She stared at the door a long moment, then forced herself up the sidewalk and knocked. Pauline pulled the door open.

"What do you want?" she asked sullenly. She stood blocking the way, not inviting Margaret in.

"I came to say—to say I was sorry," Margaret stammered.

"Who is it?" Aunt Dorothy came to the door and peered around Pauline. "Oh, Margaret." She paused. "Come in."

Margaret crowded into the small, dimly lit hall. "Aunt Dorothy, I came to . . . to apologize to you and Pauline and

Mary. I should never have said what I said to Pauline. Uncle Harold is going to be fine, really he is."

"Well, I would rather you had not told the entire school about our financial position . . . and you scared your cousins badly."

Margaret bowed her head.

"But I understand from Mary that there was some provocation. Your uncle and I should have had a talk with them sooner. It's wartime. Everyone has to make sacrifices. Your Edward and the girls' father . . ." Her voice faltered, but gathered strength. "And I understand soon there will be food rationing so we will all be in the same boat. We're not used to being on our own, the girls and I, but we'll learn. We have to so that everything is still the same when Harold gets back. I accept your apology as I am sure Pauline does."

Margaret couldn't believe her ears. Aunt Dorothy accepting her apology so calmly. Pauline, however, merely glared at her.

"Now, you better run home," Aunt Dorothy went on. "It's beginning to get dark and I would have thought today of all days you'd want to be home."

Feeling lighter, Margaret walked quickly through the darkening streets. Aunt Dorothy wasn't so bad after all. *Today of all days* . . . what had her aunt meant? A shrill train whistle brought her to a standstill. Jean! She couldn't let Jean go. She headed at a full run for the train yard, arriving in time to see a freight train slowly pull from the station. Two men with packs sprinted alongside, then jumped, grabbing the iron ladders that ran up the sides of the boxcars.

"Jean! Jean!" she shrieked.

The train whistled piercingly, then picked up speed until the cars clacked by too fast for Margaret to see inside. A caboose swept past and the train was gone. Black soot from the engine settled about Margaret's shoulders in the sudden quiet. Jean was gone. Everyone was gone. Grandma, Edward, Mama . . . their farm.

Through a blur of tears, Margaret made out a girl stepping over red iron rails. "Jean!" she yelled.

She ran to meet her friend, sweeping the girl up into a hug. "You didn't leave."

"Couldn't run fast enough to get on the train," Jean mumbled.

Margaret frowned, puzzled. Jean was a fast runner. She remembered her flying down the street when the policeman was chasing them.

"Are you going to try again?"

Jean shrugged. "Don't know."

"So here's where you got to." Allan came up to them. "Your dad's looking for you, Margaret."

"Oh, no." Margaret put a hand over her mouth. "I'd better get home. He's so mad at me right now."

"I told him you'd gone for a walk with Jean. He's talking to Mother. It seems he's offering to make her a cupboard similar to yours. They're going over the terms now, so he'll be occupied for a while." Allan assured her. He looked over at the other girl. "So you decided not to go," he said gently.

"Not right now anyway." Jean's face suddenly crumpled, tears running down her cheeks. "I was too scared to go all by myself. To jump on the train and go to Halifax."

Allan patted her shoulder awkwardly. "Being scared is fine. I'm terrified to go off to the war."

"You are?"

"Yes." He paused. "I know things haven't been good for you, Jean, but I have to believe they will get better and you do, too."

"You can't go back, so go forward with faith, love, hope, and courage," Margaret suddenly said. Then she gave an embarrassed laugh. "That's what my Grandma Brown always said." She'd almost forgotten that, fighting to go back so much, she'd stopped herself from going forward.

"Your Grandma Brown sounds like a wise woman," Allan told her. "We better get off these train tracks." He put an arm under Jean's elbow.

Jean wiped her nose with the back of her hand, and Margaret hid a grin at Allan's wince.

"I'm holding you to your promise, Margaret." Allan said. "I need you girls to watch my mother. Keep her company and write and tell me all the horrid things she says and does."

Margaret grinned at Jean, then remembered the awful words she'd flung at Mrs. Ferguson. "She might not want me visiting her anymore."

"Oh, she'll want you to visit," Allan assured her. "Mother loves crossing swords with people and you two do it best. But it'll be a paying position from now on. It's no picnic visiting Mother."

"I didn't mind," Margaret assured him. She had enjoyed the time with Jean and Mrs. Ferguson, listening to them fight while she worked on her quilt.

"Nevertheless, that's what I've decided. A paying position. Jean can save up for nursing school, and, Margaret, maybe you'll be able to get some material to finish your quilt. I'll work out the details with Mother."

"Oh." Jean reached down, grabbed the hem of her coat, and tugged hard. There was a ripping sound, then she held out a piece of black material to Margaret. "Is this any good for your quilt? I can give you more if you like," she said eagerly, reaching for the hem again.

"This is just fine, thank you," Margaret assured her hastily. Jean would tear her coat to pieces! "There'll be a remembrance of you in my quilt."

"Well, don't finish it too fast," Jean said. "I wouldn't want you leaving soon."

Margaret shook her head. "The farm isn't ours anymore. I

know that now. And I know the quilt won't take us back to Saskatchewan. That was just a foolish idea I had."

"What will you do with your quilt?" Jean asked.

"I don't know," Margaret replied.

Allan began to walk off. "Jean, I'm going to walk you home. I want to talk to your mother about the—job I'm offering you." His face momentarily darkened, then his eyes twinkled again. "And, Margaret, you better head home, as I said your father is looking for you, and someone else is, too." He smiled secretly.

"Who?" Margaret asked.

"Just go," Allan told her.

Hurrying along the streets, Margaret thought hard about her Flying Geese quilt. She had been so sure finishing it would take her back to Saskatchewan. Her feet slowed. Well, maybe it would still bring someone home. Edward. He might be in France by now, up at the front, cold and wet. She'd send him the quilt to keep him warm, and maybe in time it would bring him back to her family.

Happily, Margaret pushed open the door to the cottage, the wind catching it and slamming it with a resounding bang.

"Hush!" a soft voice said. "You'll wake the baby."

"Mama!" Margaret threw herself into her mother's arms.

Chapter 20

A gentle shake woke Margaret from a sound sleep to find her father bending over her.

"Is anything wrong?" she asked sleepily. "Mama? Baby Hope?"

"Nothing's wrong," her father assured her. "Get dressed quietly so you don't wake Evie. There's something I want to show you."

Margaret crept down the stairs in her stocking feet and paused in the kitchen to tie on her boots, smiling as she heard Baby Hope's mewling cries from her parents' bedroom and her mother's soothing voice. She followed her father out the kitchen door into the pink spring dawn. The air held a chill, but she saw the yellow of a crocus.

"Where are we going?" she asked.

"You'll see," was all she could get out of him.

They walked along quiet morning streets, past sleeping houses with curtains drawn and smoke rising in lazy blue curls from chimneys. Soon they arrived at the bridge over the river. Mr. Brown stopped halfway across. "Now watch," he said, leaning over the railing.

"What for?"

"Just watch and you'll see."

Newly yellow-green willows dipped graceful branches into red and gold sun-touched water. Brown bulrushes mingled with emerald-green growth along the banks. Suddenly,

Margaret heard a single, flat *honk*, then others joining, filling the air with sound. She squinted into the early morning sun to see geese fly low over the river. Wings beat strong and heads strained northward. Spring had arrived.

Quilting is not easy, but if you take time and patience and do the best you can, in the end it will all come together into something beautiful.

Glossary

TEMPLATE: is a pattern for quilt pieces. It is made of plastic or light-weight cardboard. You mark around it, then cut out the shape.

SEAM ALLOWANCE: is the distance between the cut edge of a fabric and the stitching line. Unless indicated otherwise, a .5 cm (¼ inch) seam allowance is always used in quilting.

BORDERS: act as a frame for the pieced blocks.

PIECING: is joining together the cut patches or pieces of material to form a pattern or block.

QUILTING: is done when the quilt top and batting and backing have been sandwiched together (a quilt sandwich). It is done with a short running stitch that goes through all layers.

TYING: is an alternative to quilting, once a quilt sandwich is made. Yarn is run through all three layers and knotted or tied. This is done evenly spaced every 7 cms.

SASHING: are the strips of materials running between the finished quilt blocks to separate and set them together to form a quilt top.

BACKING: is fabric which forms the bottom layer of the quilt.

BATTING: is the filling used between the top and the backing and provides thickness and warmth to the quilt. In the past corn husks, straw, raw cotton, old blankets and worn quilts were used. Today quilters use bonded polyester or cotton batts.

BINDING: is a narrow strip of fabric used to enclose the raw edges of the quilt sandwich.

Make Your Own
Flying Geese Coaster

I made my coaster from blue, yellow and white felt, but you can make yours from any colours you want.

YOU'LL NEED:
1 piece each of blue, yellow and white felt
a pencil
scissors
a ruler
a sheet of paper
cereal-box cardboard
white craft glue
pins
needle and thread

INSTRUCTIONS:
1 Measure and cut out a 13 cm (5 inch) large square, a 7.5 cm (3 inch) medium square, and a 6 cm (2½ inch) small square of paper.
2 Glue the squares onto a piece of cereal-box cardboard and cut them out. These are your templates.
3 Use the pencil to trace the large template onto your yellow felt and the medium template onto the blue felt. Trace the small template twice onto the white felt.

4 Cut out the four squares. Cut the blue square and the two white squares corner to corner so you now have six triangles.

5 Place the large yellow square on the table top. Line up the cut edge of one of the blue triangles about .5 cm (¼ inch) above the bottom edge of the large yellow square. Pin it in place.

6 Line up the cut edges of two of the white triangles to the two remaining edges of the blue triangle. Pin them in place.

7 Centre the cut edge of the second blue triangle above the point of the first and follow instruction 6.

8 With a needle and contrasting thread, sew a line .5 cm (¼ inch) along the inside edges of each triangle.

You now have a coaster. To make a whole set of coasters, reuse your templates. You can make a greeting card the same way out of construction or wrapping paper—use your imagination.

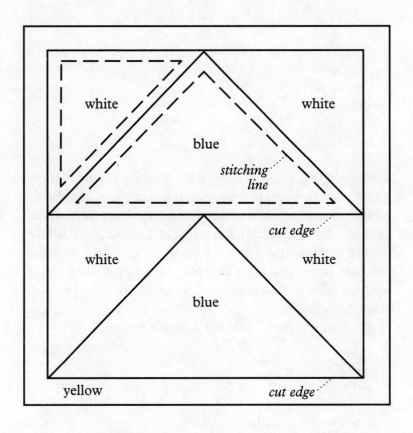

Barbara Haworth-Attard's 1997 children's book, *Home Child*, was published to great critical acclaim, including being shortlisted for the Mr. Christie Book Award; the Silver Birch Award; the Red Cedar Award; and the Geoffrey Bilson Award for Historical Fiction. Film rights have been sold and Barbara is writing the screenplay. Barbara's other books include *Dark of the Moon*, *TruthSinger* and her most recent, *Love-Lies Bleeding*.

She lives with her family in London, Ontario.